FEUD

PHYLLIS BOURNE

Red Lipstick Press
REDLIPSTICKPRESS.COM

1

"The only good Bridges is a dead one."

JUSTICE

TODAY'S THE DAY.

Padding barefoot into the kitchen, I bypassed the coffeemaker and made a beeline for the calendar stuck to the refrigerator door. An unbroken chain of *x's* marked the boxes leading up to today – a date I'd circled in red six-months ago when the son-of-a-bitch next door dropped dead.

Yeah, I realize how awful that sounds, but you can miss me with the judgmental attitude.

The late Tate Alexander Bridges had been more than

a pain in my ass. The miserable old bastard had also been the last of the Bridges clan, and his taking a dirt nap at the ripe old age of ninety-seven via heart attack ended the most infamous feud between neighbors in Tennessee history.

What was the long-running feud over?

Don't ask. But at its height, folks said the bad blood between the Bridges and the Lawson families made the legendary Hatfield-McCoy feud look like a playground squabble.

I'm Justice, last of the Lawson clan, and six-months with no Bridges heir on the horizon also makes me the feud's and Old Trail Avenue's soul survivor. I grabbed the red pen attached to the calendar and slashed an *x* thru today's date. Satisfied, I went to the sink to fill the coffee carafe with water and peered through the window at the vacant house next door.

Lawsons – 1

Bridges – 0

A fist pounded against the back door before I could break into the family feud equivalent of a celebratory touchdown dance. I yanked it open. It could only be one person. The same one who'd banged on the back door of this house since we were kids and he'd lived across the street.

"What's cooking, playa?" Ned Dixon stepped into the kitchen, the newspaper from my front porch tucked under his arm. He sniffed the air and then froze. Frowning, his eyes flicked from the empty kitchen table to the cold stove. "What's up with breakfast?"

I pulled a bag of coffee from the cabinet and dumped a scoopful of grounds into the coffeemaker filter basket. "There's cereal in the pantry."

"Cereal?" Ned asked incredulous as if I'd just insulted his mama. "How do you expect me to eat Frosted Flakes, when I've been spoiled with cinnamon French toast, banana-coconut pancakes and those buttermilk waffles you make with crisp bacon or those..."

I switched on the coffeemaker as Ned continued. My childhood friend parking his behind at my kitchen table was one of those things I filed under shit you start as a one-off and it somehow turns into routine. Actually, my grandma started it back when this was her house. Ned would stop by to check on her while I was in Europe, and she fed him on the regular.

When Grandma got sick, I moved back into the house she'd raised me in and put my Parisian culinary degree to work tempting her to eat when the last thing she'd wanted was food.

"How about whipping up some cheesy eggs, cheese grits, cheese toast or..." Ned continued, still standing in the middle of the kitchen staring pitifully at the stove.

Nowadays my friend more or less served as a guinea pig, and I tried out recipes to determine which would make the menu of the breakfast-only café I intended to open in New York City with money I hoped to receive as early as today.

"Or maybe one of those egg pies," Ned continued. "What do you call them again?" He snapped his fingers before answering his own question. "Quiche. Yeah, quiche. Can't you whip up one right quick?"

"Not today."

The coffeemaker gurgled, signaling the end of the brewing cycle.

"But—"

I cut off Ned's protest. "You knew this was all going to come to an end, right?"

"Yeah, but I didn't think I'd have to go back to the drive-thru until you could claim the cash on that weird feud clause in your Grandma's will," he said.

I inclined my head toward the calendar on the fridge.

"Damn, that's today?" Ned asked.

I nodded. My new life began today.

"So it's official, huh?" Ned asked the rhetorical question and blew out a low whistle. "You're the last man standing in the Bridges-Lawson feud."

I hoisted the mug I'd just filled with coffee. "My ancestor's wildest dream."

Ned snorted and cast a glance in the direction of the house next door. "I'll bet old man Bridges is spinning in his grave like a rotisserie chicken."

Following his gaze, I looked out the window at the house next door, a circa 1920s shotgun shack that, except for its yellow exterior looked exactly liked this one. "You can bet wherever Bridges is right now there's a flame beneath his ass."

"Come on. He wasn't *that* bad," Ned chuckled. "Well, except when it came to your family. Remember that block party?"

I remembered. It had been back when Old Trail Avenue could still be considered a block. Back when Ned's family still lived across the street. Before their home and half the houses on the other side of the street had been erased by a tornado in the 1990s. And before fierce storm seasons chipped away at the rest of the houses on this block until only two remained standing, both as stubborn as their occupants.

I made a mental note to make a Home Depot run for roof shingles sooner rather than later. I'd already *long-term borrowed* old man Bridges extension ladder from his unlocked shed. *Oh, come on.* It wasn't like he was using it, and my ladder didn't extend long enough to reach the roof.

Ah, but back to the block party. It had started out great. Everyone had chipped in, neighbors providing food and cold drinks. Adults chatted and listened to music as they watched their children play games in the blocked-off street. The Lawsons and Bridges had even managed to avoid each other's company.

It wasn't until a five-year old Ned reached into a cooler for a grape-flavored Popsicle and made the mistake of giving me a cherry one that all hell broke loose.

"Mr. Bridges snatched that Popsicle out of your hand so hard, I thought he'd taken one of your fingers," Ned reminisced. "No stinking Lawson is going to suck on a Popsicle I bought, and I don't care if he is only a snot-nosed kid."

"Stop it, before you make coffee spew out of my snotnose." Laughing, I held up a hand. I'll be damned if Ned didn't sound just like my late neighbor.

Ned pulled a mug from the cabinet and filled it with coffee. "Your grandma got in his face, and I'd seriously believed they were gonna throw hands."

"Yeah, grandma was the epitome of a black Southern belle until she heard the name Bridges." A bittersweet smile tugged at the corner of my mouth. When it came to the Bridges, the woman who'd raised me was always in one of two modes - bitching about Tate Bridges latest salvo in the ongoing family feud or plotting how she'd retaliate.

Ned dumped two teaspoons of sugar in his coffee, leaned against the other end of the counter, and took a sip. "They both took that old feud seriously, that's for sure. Until their dying days."

By now, you're *really* itching to know what started the feud all those decades ago. Again, I'd prefer not to get into it, but I will answer another question undoubtedly running through your mind.

Why does it still have legs?

Pretty much the same reason the rumor mill continuously churned. Every generation heaped fuel on the flames and instilled the ongoing fight in their offspring, giving the feud new life. So any talk of a truce had been lost on grandma, who'd made it clear that the lessons in forgiveness and good citizenship I'd learned in school and church applied to everyone, *except the Bridges.*

I'll answer one last question while Ned rustles

through the pantry in search of Pop-Tarts, and I polish off my coffee.

Why didn't you put an end to this feud business after your grandmother passed on?

Ha. I tried. First of all, I couldn't relate to the age-old incident that caused the feud, and as a reasonable, grown-assed man, I didn't harbor a grudge against old man Bridges for his Popsicle pettiness. So the day after grandma's funeral I made my first trip ever next door determined to forge a truce.

If you're still with me, you already know it didn't go well. So I'll summarize, instead of wasting your time with a blow-by-blow recounting.

Tate Bridges told me to get my ass off his porch before he got his shotgun. Propped up by a cane, I doubted the man could lift the toilet seat, never mind a shotgun, but that didn't stop him from talking shit. After several attempts to get through to him, I gave up and started for home.

"Hey, Lawson," Bridges had yelled to my retreating back as I crossed his driveway back to my yard. "Old Trail Avenue ain't big enough for the both of us. So I'm saving a bottle of vintage champagne for the day I succeed in either running you out of that shack next door or you croak and join your kinfolk in hell. I don't care which one, because either will leave me a rich man."

I hadn't understood what he'd meant by that last cryptic crack. Not until the following week when I sat in a lawyer's office for the reading of Grandma's will. As her only living relative, I'd expected her modest estate would be passed down to me. However, there had also been a special clause in the will – one that had been handed down through generations. It had been nicknamed the *feud clause*. The Lawson that managed to convince the Bridges to sell the house next door or outlived that blasted family would inherit money that had been collecting interest for nearly a hundred years. The account that money rested in now had a balance of nearly two hundred and fifty thousand dollars.

Not to be outdone by the Lawsons the Bridges came up with a similar feud clause attached to an even bigger bank account. Fortunately for me, old Tate Bridges would never collect on it.

Ned emerged from the pantry grumbling about having to settle for a protein bar. He gave the one he'd unwrapped a sniff before taking a tentative bite. "Man, this tastes like chalk." That didn't keep him from taking another bite. "How do you eat this shit?"

I poured the remainder of my coffee down the drain. "Can't stand around talking all day. Gotta get dressed so I can head downtown to the lawyer's office and handle my business."

Ned polished off the protein bar in one bite. "Alright then." He eased off the counter he'd been resting against. "I'll catch you later, *big money*."

"Man, get out of here with that." Although I'd hoped the paperwork would be processed quickly enough that by the end of the week big money would indeed be sitting in my bank account.

At the door, Ned hesitated. "You pulling your shift at

the bar tonight or will you be too busy packing to get out of dodge?"

"I'll be there," I assured my friend.

However, once my final inheritance replenished my depleted bank account, I would indeed pack and get the hell out of dodge.

2

"If it lies, cheats, or steals, it's a Lawson."

ALEX

"HELL, YEAH!"

My spontaneous yell bounced off the staid wood-panel walls. The gleeful shout as inappropriate at the reading of a will as the fist pump that accompanied it.

Don't start with the judging. Trust me, I'm getting plenty stink-eye from the attorney glaring at me over the wire-rimmed glasses perched on his nose. Guess he's never been broke, and I don't mean the 'let me hold a couple of dollars until payday' kind of broke.

I'm talking empty Louis Vuitton bag, cleaned out bank account, don't know how I'll make next month's rent kind of broke. Again, don't start. The Louis Vuitton ships to the highest bidder on eBay at the end of the week.

In fact, the only reason I was able to catch an early morning flight to Nashville for an overdue reading of a great, great-uncle's will was a short-term loan from my mom, who like me, hadn't realized I'd even had an uncle. Still, a warning came with the temporary use of her credit card. "Don't get your hopes up, honey," Mom cautioned after she'd read off her card number and expiration date over the phone. "I loved your father, Lord rest his soul, but that family of his were a bunch of lunatics. I wouldn't be surprised if they left you a pet skunk."

Mom had been wrong.

As in my late uncle had left me *a house and a modest savings account, wrong*. I've clued you in on my current situation, so I'm sure you'll pardon me for reacting like I'd won the Powerball.

The attorney, apparently over my inappropriate exuberance, continued. "It's an old house. Built by your family in the early 1920s, so it's small by today's standards."

It could be one of those ridiculous tiny houses that rich folks claimed to live in on HGTV for all I cared. Honestly, I believed those toy houses were situated in the backyards of the six thousand square foot homes they truly lived in.

Anyway, back to *my* house. This was one of the few situations where size didn't matter. (They'll try to tell you it doesn't matter in the bedroom, but trust me, it does.)

After being forced out of my job, my living options for the next month had dwindled to moving in with mom, her second husband, and my rambunctious half-brothers, or pushing a shopping cart filled with my possessions up and down the NYC sidewalks.

I loved living in New York, but if having a free and clear roof over my head meant a temporary move south, so be it. I desperately needed a place to regroup and plot my comeback after leaving my job of the last five years.

"Ms. Bridges..."

I blinked. The sound of my name yanked me from a daydream where I was about to squeeze my hands around my former boss's throat. Come on now, if your boss had led you to believe you were getting a promotion and screwed you over instead, you'd fantasize about choking the shit out of him too.

"Alex or Alexandra is fine," I said automatically. My first name was more suited for a frontier cowboy, and I avoided using it whenever possible.

Straightening in the chair positioned on the other side of the attorney's desk, I forced myself to focus as he informed me that the house's furnishings had been left to a veteran's organization. There was more, but it got lost in the legalese and monotone delivery. The word 'confused' must have appeared in a thought bubble above my head, because my uncle's attorney paused.

"Why don't we just move on to the video your uncle left for you, it should..."

Huh? I'm sure another thought bubble popped up over my head. "But he didn't even know I existed."

Holding a DVD, the elderly man shuffled toward the television on the other side of his office. "Mr. Bridges thought his great nephew had mentioned a pregnancy or a child, but after much of his family died so tragically he wasn't sure if it was a memory or wishful thinking." The attorney slid a disc into the player. "He came into the office a few days before he died to ask us to start a search. Mr. Bridges also recorded this video in case we located an heir."

The hairs on the back of my neck tingled as the image of an elderly man sitting at the head of a conference table appeared on the screen. I was broke (and admittedly, a little greedy), but the moment wasn't lost on me. This video was my first and only connection to my father's side of the family. It was also a faint familial thread to the dad that I'd lost, along with much of his family, in a plane crash on their way to a family reunion.

They say you don't miss what you never had, but that's a lie. There isn't a day that goes by that I don't glance at the old photograph of my smiling father, forever young and frozen in time, and wonder *what if?*

That's so sad.

Chill with the waterworks. I don't need your pity. My mom and her family picked up the slack as best they could. Besides, I never heard of tears bringing anyone back. You?

Um....

Exactly. So why bother?

"Is that thing on?" The old man on the screen raised a gnarled finger to point at what I assumed was the camera, while I examined his face on the high definition monitor. Marred by wrinkles, my namesake's face had nothing in common with mine. His skin was dark, not the color of wheat fields beneath the summer sun. Nor was he covered in the huge freckles that had earned me the dreaded childhood nickname of *101 Dalmatians*.

Standing, I walked toward the monitor for a closer look. I didn't know what I was searching for until I saw it in his eyes. *Resemblance*. Beneath the straggly gray eyebrows and cataract clouds, his light brown eyes were just like the father's I'd only seen in photographs *and mine*.

"*Gotdammit!*"

My great, great uncle's bellow took me by surprise, and I nearly jumped out of my skin. I blinked at the screen as those eyes bore into me. If I didn't know better, I'd swear my uncle's wrath was directed at me. Yes, I'm well aware of how ridiculous that sounds. Again, Mom always said those Bridges were lunatics, and my last name *is* Bridges.

"Well, is it on or not?" My uncle barked and then nodded once apparently satisfied. "Good. I want to get this over with. I've got a hankering for a Chick-fil-a sammich, and you know that place turns into a zoo if you wait around until noon. Cars swarming the parking lot like they were giving away bags of free money."

A female voice in the background reminded him that he was indeed being recorded.

My uncle cleared his throat. "I'm Tate Alexander Bridges. Well, if you're watching this I'm the *late* Tate

Bridges. But you can bet I'm sitting on a cloud in the great beyond with a shit-eating grin on my face right now, because if you're watching this there is indeed a Bridges heir." He threw his head back and laughed. "*Oooooh, wee!* I'd give anything to see the look on that snot-nosed Lawson's face when he finds out. Bet that arrogant fucker thought he'd outlived us."

The elderly man on the screen broke into more gravelly laughter that morphed into a coughing fit.

"Lawson?" I turned to the attorney.

My uncle's representative inclined his head toward the monitor, where the same woman who had shown me into this office earlier was handing my uncle a glass of water. "Your uncle explains everything," he said.

I turned back to the monitor as the man on the screen noisily slurped from the glass.

Then the attorney cleared his throat. "Ms. Bridges, uh, I mean Alexandra," he began.

Still standing, I looked over my shoulder. The attorney had rounded his desk and was moving the chair I'd been sitting in toward me.

"I think you'd better have a seat." His expression added *cause you're going to need it.*

He was right.

I spent the next ten minutes listening as my great, great-uncle gave me a family history lesson from the grave. Apparently, the Bridges have been fighting with their neighbors the Lawson's for decades. I'll tell ya. Mom was gonna love hearing about this. She was definitely the *told you so type.* And on the crazy meter, a feud that sounded straight out of the Old West ranked higher than her suspected pet skunk.

"I can't believe they've been fighting about that for so long," I said when Tate Bridges paused for another drink of water. "I mean, nobody even uses ..."

The attorney shrugged. "Mules were considered very valuable back then."

Still, you'd think a subsequent generation of Bridges and Lawsons would have put an end to it. I rolled my eyes. Feuds are *sooooo* eighteenth century.

On screen, my uncle put down his empty water glass, swiped the back of his hand across his mouth and asked for the time. "Dang it! It's past noon, and I'm not even done explaining everything," he grumbled. "Now I'll be stuck eating at that hot chicken joint. No matter how many times I tell them mild, they soak the bird in red pepper. Ate there last month and shit flames for a week."

Ew. I closed my eyes briefly as if it would block that image from my brain and made a mental note to pass on Nashville's famous hot chicken. Squirming in my seat, I cast a surreptitious glance at my watch. This had been an entertaining tale so far, but I had a house I was eager to see. Besides, what did that ridiculous old feud have to do with me?

I must have uttered the question aloud.

"Your uncle's getting to that part," the attorney assured.

I focused on the screen as my elderly ancestor revealed a clause that had been in the last wills and testaments of Bridges family members for decades. He called it the *feud clause*. Apparently, there was a bank account that, thanks to the power of compound interest, now had a balance of over three hundred thousand dollars.

"Good gracious," I gasped.

My math-challenged brain turned into a cash register as I mentally calculated what I could do with that kind of money. I'd be able to keep up the rent on my apartment while I found a new job or even better, started my own advertising agency.

"Slow your greedy roll, young 'un." My uncle's raspy chuckle filled the room. "Don't get ahead of yourself. You may be holding a lottery ticket, but you ain't won, *yet*. So listen up and listen good."

Uh, oh. I don't know about you, but I'm starting to think my mom was right after all and there was a pet skunk waiting in the wings. That kind of money sitting untouched by generations of Bridges, there has to be a catch, right?

My uncle continued, detailing what would have to happen before all that money could be transferred to my personal account. The more he talked, the more it seemed like babysitting a skunk would have been easier. I mean what kind of people thought up convoluted shit like this? My mom's voice echoed in my head, *'lunatics'*.

"The good news is there's only one Lawson left, unless he's knocked up some broad," my uncle said.

What am I supposed to do, shoot him?

"I thought about shooting him." My uncle's cackle once again filled the room. "But I'm still too good-looking for jail."

So am I.

The old man on the screen rubbed at the gray stubble along his chin. "But there are two other ways to get that money, and the fact that you're watching this confirms neither of them worked for me. Maybe you'll have better luck."

By now, I figured my great, great uncle was either a bit demented or bat-shit crazy. Still, I was all-ears and the tip of my nose practically touched the monitor.

"You can keep an eye on the weather. Mother Nature took out every other house on the street, but no matter how much I wished she'd send a tornado or lightening bolt to destroy that Lawson shack, it never happened. You see, if they don't have a house, the money will be released to you immediately." My uncle leaned in as if he were about to divulge a secret. "By the way, there's a gas can and matches in the shed. Thought about using them once or twice, but that whole jail thing."

My shoulder's slumped a notch as I pushed out a sigh. *Shit*. If these suggestions were my best shot, odds were I'd never see a dime of that money either.

"But you probably aren't finding those suggestions very helpful," he said as if he'd read my mind.

You think? I silently asked the old man on the screen.

"So your best bet is to run him out," my uncle said. "Tried to do it myself, until old age crept up on me. But hopefully, you'll have enough get up left in you to make Lawson's life so miserable, he'll leave that house and the great state of Tennessee, *forever*."

Now *that* idea had merit.

I know what you're thinking; *she's as crazy as the rest of her people*. But it's only crazy when you're broke. Three hundred thousand dollars is enough to buy my way up to the much better sounding *eccentric*.

Ideas for how to rid myself of a neighbor I'd never even met popped into my head as my uncle listed some more of the things he'd tried. A few months ago, I would have dismissed the notion as absurd, but that was before working hard and doing the right thing had earned me a swift kick in my naively loyal ass.

"You'd think that hag next door would have been scared out of her dentures." My uncle's voice broke into my thoughts. "Nope. Old lady Lawson just picked up that snake I'd left on her porch and flung it across the driveway onto my doorstep."

He rattled off a few more of his attempts to run the Lawsons out of their house before either hunger or exhaustion won over. "Well, it's all up to you now, and regardless of the fact that you're the last of us, family still comes first." The elderly man jabbed a finger in the air, and I jerked as if it had actually touched my chest. "Don't you forget it, young Bridges, *or I'll find my way back from wherever I am to remind you*."

The hairs on the back of my neck rose at his threat, and I rubbed at the gooseflesh erupting on my bare arms.

Then I came to my senses.

"*Lunatic*," I muttered under my breath.

Yeah, your mom does have a point.

Ha! You're telling me.

The jingle of keys caught my attention, and I looked back at the attorney.

He slid the keys across the desk. "The house keys." He extended a pen in my direction. "There are a few documents that require your signature, then you can be on your way."

A knock sounded at the door as I signed the last of the paperwork, and the assistant who'd shown me in earlier cracked the door just wide enough to stick her head inside the office. She looked past me at the attorney. "Sorry to interrupt, but..."

"Can it wait, Susan?" the attorney asked.

She cast a pointed look in my direction, before shaking her head.

Sighing deeply, the attorney excused himself and left the room, closing the door behind him. I heard the rumble of voices outside the door, before it swung open again. My uncle's attorney walked in. "There's someone here I think you should meet."

I looked past the attorney; my gaze riveted to the man behind him whose broad shoulders filled the doorway.

He stood tall enough to carry the breadth of those shoulders with ease, and his skin was reminiscent of dark chocolate buttercream on a cake that looked too perfect to eat. My tongue slid over my bottom lip.

The man was absolutely yummy.

Clearing his throat, the lawyer appeared nervous as his gaze shifted from me and then back to what had to be one of the absolute finest men I'd ever laid eyes on.

"Tate Bridges, meet Justice Lawson."

3

"If you're depending on a Bridges to screw up a good day,
you won't be disappointed."

JUSTICE

"Beg your pardon?" I asked aloud, while I silently
yelled, *what the fuck?*

Then I realized this was some kind of elaborate prac-
tical joke. Yup. That had to be it.

First of all, the last Bridges had checked out six-
months ago, *good riddance*, and secondly, no way a
woman as stunning as this one could be kin to Tate
Bridges, let alone bear the same name as that old goat.

Besides, she didn't look anything like him, I reassured
myself, taking in the sweet, heart-shaped face covered by

a more than generous helping of freckles. Her mouth was painted a shade of hot pink as bold as the flecks of brown covering her café au lait hue. She blinked, drawing my gaze to her eyes.

Uh, oh.

You got that right, because I knew those light brown eyes. They were just like the ones that flashed with hostility whenever my late neighbor had looked my way. Then she confirmed what I'd already surmised to be true.

"Tate *Alexandra* Bridges." Those hot pink lips spread into a smile that was both bright and engaging. "I go by Alexandra or just plain ..." She stopped abruptly. "Wait a minute. Did he say your name was *Lawson?*" Her smile dimmed, and then vanished as understanding dawned.

I turned to my grandmother's lawyer, who was standing behind me avoiding my gaze. "You couldn't pick up the phone?" Before I drove down here, expecting to leave a quarter of a million dollars richer.

She shrugged and gave me a bullshit excuse. Her partner glanced at his watch. "I'm going to treat myself to one of those milkshake coffee drinks over at the Starbucks. In the meantime, you two are welcome to use my office to continue your conversation."

"I could use a strong cup of joe," Grandma's attorney said, as if she'd been the one blindsided by the appearance of a Bridges this morning.

"And keep it civil you two," Her partner warned. "I don't want a repeat of what happened the last time a Bridges and a Lawson were in the same room. Tear up my office, and I won't hesitate to send you both the bill."

Finally, they left and shut the door behind them.

"*Jerks.*" The insult popped out of our mouths simultaneously, marking the first time a Bridges and a Lawson had agreed on anything in decades.

Consider it an opportunity to do the right thing and end the feud, just like you've always wanted.

You're right. As a modern, intelligent, levelheaded man, I needed to swallow my disappointment and extend an olive branch. It's what should have been done generations ago, what I'd attempted to do with stubborn old man Bridges. This feud was idiotic and had already gone on far too long. I took a deep breath and slowly released it.

You can do it.

Appreciate the vote of confidence.

"So you're old man Bridges..." I began.

"I'm his great, great niece." She filled in the blank.

"I'd thought your uncle didn't have any family left."

A corner of her pink slicked mouth ticked upwards. "Up until the other day, I hadn't even known my uncle existed," she said. "Fortunately, his attorney tracked me down."

Yeah, fortunately. "And I'm assuming you know the history between our families."

Leaning against the desk, Alexandra (cause in my mind there was still only one Tate Bridges) inclined her head toward a television monitor where her late uncle's mean face was frozen on the screen. "Got it straight from the horse's mouth."

I glanced down at the keys in her hand. "You

intending to move into the house you apparently just inherited?"

"Most definitely." She raised a perfectly arched brow. "What's it to you?"

Let's pause right here, seeing at how we've come to the proverbial fork in the road. The way I see it, this situation can go one of two ways. I could continue to fight this dumb assed feud or try once again to put an end to it. I could welcome Alexandra Bridges as my neighbor. Maybe even invite her to my place and prepare a brunch spread that would have her clawing at my back door every morning (or maybe just clawing at my back).

"You look like a nice woman," I said.

So far, so good. You're doing great. Now follow thru.

"Walk away, and go back where you came from." The wrong words tumbled out of my mouth.

You don't have to say anything, because I already know what you're thinking. Like generations of Lawson's before me, the ones that I'd referred to as immature and ridiculous whenever grandma had been out of earshot, just like them, I'd stirred up the shit I should have been putting to rest.

But there was an untouched two hundred and fifty thousand dollar Lawson bank account that I was still hoping to get my hands on.

"Hmmm," Alexandra murmured, appearing to consider my warning. However, a spark of annoyance in her light brown eyes said different.

"Trust me, ma'am. This isn't a fight you want."

Pushing off the desk she'd been leaning against, she

toed up to me. "My late uncle just informed me that there's a Bridges bank account with three-hundred thousand dollars in it, just waiting on me. All I have to do to get it is outlive you or run you out of that house next door."

"Then you should know I have similar incentive to be the neighbor from hell," I said, in a tone so menacing I barely recognized it as my own. Ditto for my asshole behavior.

Damn woman didn't as much as flinch.

"I'll keep that in mind."

"Suit yourself, but you can also keep in mind that pretty face of yours won't stop me from getting down and dirty." I took a step forward. "Because all I'll ever see when I look at you is a Bridges."

She shrugged nonchalantly, as if I'd given her the weather report. "It's also the face of a woman who's recently been screwed over and hasn't had anyone to take it out on." Raising a finger, she aimed it at my chest. "So make your move, Lawson, because I have a few moves of my own."

———

NED'S LAUGHTER filled the empty bar as he locked the front door and switched off the neon OPEN sign.

"It's not funny." I grunted, and then grumbled under my breath.

The fact was all I'd done since I'd started my evening shift at my friend's sports bar was grunt and grumble. I'd grumbled as I filled the ice bins. Grunted while I'd sliced fruit to garnish cocktails with enough force to chop down an oak. I grunted and grumbled my way through six hours of mixing, shaking, and pouring drinks, not letting up as I went through my routine of closing out my register, loading glassware into the dishwasher, and wiping down the bar.

"Come on, man." Ned's laughter died down to a chuckle. "*Another Tate Bridges?* Where's your sense of humor?"

I grunted. "Guess it flew out the window, along with the two hundred fifty thousand dollars, I thought would be resting in my bank account right now."

Rounding the bar, Ned unscrewed the cap off two Heinekens. He nudged me with an elbow and handed me one. After a night of slinging drinks the thought of alcohol was usually unappealing, but I took a long swallow from the bottle.

Ned took a seat on the other side of the bar and raised his beer in mock salute. "The friend in me feels for you, man, but I'm glad you'll be sticking around for a while. "

"No choice." My restaurateur plans were on hold, *for now*.

"I know you haven't asked for advice—" Ned began.

I cut him off. "Because I don't want any."

But he's your best friend.

Yeah, and his advice is usually shit.

Ned continued hell-bent on tossing in his two cents anyway. "Well, if you ask me, you should use this time to focus on upping your breakfast game. Fine tune your menu, while you figure out how to come up with the money to finance your restaurant."

Come up with the money, *again*.

Just so you know, I'd returned to Nashville with a six-figure bank account filled with dough I busted my ass making. But medication is expensive. Especially the experimental kind my grandma's insurance and Medicare denied. It ate up my life's savings quicker than a killer shark gobbling up a bikini-clad chick in a horror flick. No regrets though. Those precious extra months of life those treatments provided had been worth more than any amount of money.

I took another swig from my beer. When Ned paused for a breath, I called him on his bullshit. "Every dish on my menu is already perfect and you know it." From the breakfast tacos with a spicy turkey chorizo to my red velvet waffles stuffed with cream cheese, each recipe had been painstakingly honed to perfection. Eyes narrowed, I grunted. "You're just looking to keep up your gourmet breakfast routine."

Ned shrugged. "Can't blame me for trying."

"You could learn to cook."

A confused expression blanketed his features as if I'd suggested he bone up on quantum physics, then he laughed and shook his head. "Nah, that's not me, bro."

"Don't knock it. My cooking game has dropped more panties than a smooth line and swagger. Women love a man that knows his way around a Viking range almost as much as the dick."

Ned's eyes widened, as he appeared to think it over,

then narrowed. "Then how come I haven't encountered any well-fed women staggering out of your back door?"

I reminded him I lived in my grandmother's house.

"Your house." Ned corrected, and then raised a brow. "Still hung up on your ex?"

"Nah." That ship had sailed when the girlfriend I'd been positive was *the one*, so positive I'd been carrying an engagement ring in my pocket waiting for the perfect moment to propose, wanted me to toss the woman who'd raise me in a nursing home. "Nothing's caught my eye."

Okay, okay. I know you're shaking your head right now and thinking I'm full of it. Someone *had* caught my attention. Freckles, bold pink lips and a mass of kinky hair that refused to be styled or tamed.

I won't lie to you and say I hadn't been attracted, but that had been before I caught her name. Just my luck, she's a fucking Bridges.

The sound of Ned clearing his throat pulled me out of my head.

"The dazed look on your face says the opposite." He stared at me a moment, and I could see the wheels turning in his head. "So she's hot, huh?"

Tilting the beer bottle toward my mouth, I played dumb. "Who?"

Ned chuckled. "Don't play dumb. *Ms.* Tate Bridges."

I shrugged a shoulder. "She's a'ight."

"Hmm, mmm."

"Okay, so she's a helluva lot more than alright," I admitted. "But she's not so fine it makes me forget her presence cost me over two hundred fifty thousand dollars *or her last name.*"

Ned circled the bar and helped himself to another beer. He lived in the two-bedroom apartment above his business, so it wasn't like he had to drive. "Again, tough break on the dough. Still, despite the showdown you and she had at the lawyer's office, you can still do what you say you've always wanted – *put an end to the feud.*"

My friend threw out terms like a neighborly and mature adult as he rounded the bar and propped a hip on a stool across from me. "You always said it was ridiculous that it had gone on as long as it had and vowed you would never behave like your grandma and old man Bridges or like you apparently did this morning."

Everything Ned said was right. So how come I wasn't feeling his sensible message to let it go? I thought back to the flash of annoyance on Alex's face as she shot daggers in my direction this morning.

I'd been just as pissed as she'd been, but my dick hadn't got the message. It had been interested. Fortunately, the head attached to my shoulders was always in control and money took precedence over pussy.

"So again, I'm going to offer you some advice," Ned continued.

Again, unwanted.

"On the day she moves in, whip up a basketful of those featherlight sweet potato biscuits drenched in your grandma's preserves and take them next door." He licked his lips. "Trust me. One taste will not only put an end to this hillbilly feud, you'll have that Bridges woman wrapped around your little finger."

I didn't want Alexandra Bridges wrapped around my finger. I wanted her speeding away from the house next door vowing never to return.

"So where's she moving here from?" Ned asked.

I shrugged. "New York City, I think."

Ned blew out a low whistle. "That's quite a haul. When is she moving in?"

"Dunno." I shrugged again, as a plan began to take shape in my head.

"Uh, oh." Ned chuckled. "I've seen the same look on your grandma's face. You definitely aren't thinking up ways to welcome Ms. Bridges to the neighborhood."

"Oh, but I am." The corners of my mouth lifted into what felt like a genuine smile.

Ned's eyes narrowed. "Then why am I getting a vibe that whatever's going through your head right now, your neighbor isn't gonna like it?"

I left my friend's question hanging in the air unanswered, but I'll confirm what you've undoubtedly already figured out. Alexandra Bridges wasn't going to like living next door to me, *not one bit*.

4

"The good book says to love your neighbor.
No one in it moved next door to a Lawson."

ALEX

ELBOW GREASE, lemon-scented cleansers and fresh air drifting through the open windows chased away the smell of old man permeating the two-bedroom bungalow that now belonged to me.

After packing up the Manhattan apartment I could no longer afford, I'd put my belongings on a moving van and took a flight to Chicago, where my mother lived with my stepfather and my younger brothers. I hadn't returned to Nashville until late last night. Mom had helped me drive my car, which had been parked in her garage the last five years.

We'd shown up at my inherited home before dawn this morning with an arsenal of cleaning products and had spent the last few hours scrubbing, dusting and polishing in preparation for the moving van's arrival later today. I'd taken kitchen and bathrooms duty and cajoled my mom into cleaning the bedrooms. We tackled the living and dining rooms together.

My mother switched off the vacuum and heaved a long, drawn out sigh. "I didn't come down here to play housekeeper, *Tate Alexandra*."

I knew where she was headed with this. However, the fact that she'd uttered my seldom-used first name kept me from breaking off some backtalk. Giving your mother lip after she addresses you by your government name is a quick way to get that lip fattened. You know what I'm talking about. So I kept my trap shut even after she reminded me yet again why she'd come.

"I'm here to keep you from buying into this ridiculous feud business and showing your ass again with that neighbor of yours."

"But he started it." I followed her into the kitchen sounding more like a petulant pre-teen than an adult. "He said—"

"You already told me," she interrupted. "I don't care what he said." Mom tossed an empty bottle of Pine-Sol in the trashcan followed by two disposable dusters caked with cobwebs.

"But you haven't even met him, you don't know what an— "

My mother cut me off again. "It doesn't matter. He's going to be your neighbor. Your only one, since there are only two houses on this street. Be the bigger person, dear. Act like the woman I raised you to be." Her voice trailed off, and I could have sworn she muttered *instead of like your lunatic family.*

Mom's mind was made up. I was wasting my time trying to make her listen to reason. Odds were we'd run into that troll next door today, and she'd see for herself.

Okay, a fine assed troll that stood well over six feet tall if there was such a thing. The fact that he'd pissed me off hadn't blinded me. However, the moment he parted those soft looking lips of his and words spewed out of his pie hole, Mom would see what I was dealing with. Then I'd probably have to stop her from breaking off her foot in his behind.

My mother peered inside the spotless, but empty fridge. "I didn't come here to starve either."

We'd swung through the twenty-four hour McDonald's drive-thru for a pre-dawn breakfast, but hours of cleaning had my stomach grumbling too. I pulled a Snickers bar from my purse, which was sitting on the counter. I tore off the wrapper and broke it in half. "Can you hold out until the movers get here? They should be here within the hour."

"I guess." Mom snatched the proffered candy and gobbled it up in two bites.

"How about I treat you to Waffle House when

they're done?" I offered. "It shouldn't take them long to unload and set up." Those movers had better not take long seeing as my funds were limited, and I was paying by the hour once their truck hit my curb.

"Make it that country café that's known for its biscuits and gravy, and we have a deal. My neighbor Mona, you know Mona, had a work conference in Nashville, and she raved about their melt-in-your-mouth biscuits for weeks. She even brought me a nice souvenir mug." She paused long enough to give me a pointed look. "That's how neighbors *are supposed* to behave."

The rumble of an approaching truck in the distance kept me from responding with the fact that while Mona was a lovely person, Justice Lawson's good looks and hot body were wasted on a jackass. A jackass that was costing me three hundred thousand dollars.

"We'll hit up the Loveless Café for biscuits and gravy as soon as the movers are done," I called out, running to the front of the house.

Sure enough, I peered thru the living room's freshly cleaned picture window to see an eighteen-wheeler from Snappy Movers coming to a stop in front of the house. I met the rotund driver at the curb as he climbed down from the truck's cab, belly first.

"Morning, ma'am." He swiped at the tablet he was holding and glanced up. "Looking for Tate Bridges, he around?"

"I'm Tate."

He blinked, but quickly recovered, and a rumble sounded from the direction of his stomach. "Last night's thunderstorms slowed me down, and I had to push through to make up the lost time. Missed breakfast."

What was up with hungry folks whining to me about their breakfast situation this morning?

He stuck out his hand. "Anyway, I'm Joe and we're happy you chose Snappy for your relocation needs."

His stomach growled louder, but my eyes were on the truck as I gave his hand a brief shake. It had taken me, and the few friends that hadn't abandoned me once I'd lost my job, two days to pack up my apartment. How was hungry assed Joe going to get it all off that truck? And seeing as though he was being paid by the hour, how long was it going to take him?

"Just you?" I asked.

Joe shook his head. "Company contracted some local guys to help me unload." He looked down at the tablet computer again. "According to the GPS, they're less than a minute away."

Just then a pick-up rolled up the street in our direction and parked behind the moving van. The two burly men inside ambled toward where Joe and I were standing. Yeah, ambled as in moving too slow for folks that were currently on my dime.

They mumbled sleep deprived morning greetings.

"You boys didn't happen to stop for donuts and maybe have one or two in your truck?" Joe asked, and then promptly launched into a rehash about last night's storms and his empty stomach.

"No time. Lightning knocked out the power at my place so I overslept." One of the men from the pick-up rubbed his stomach. "Buddy and I were hoping the nice lady here had set up a little continental breakfast."

Three pairs of eyes stared at me hopefully.

Were they freaking serious?

I glanced at my watch. Time was money, *my money*, and they'd wasted at least five minutes of it yapping about shit that wasn't my concern.

"The sooner the three of you get busy unloading my things off that rig and get them set up in that house, which by the way I don't see a restaurant sign on the front porch, the sooner you can get out of here." I narrowed my gaze as I scanned their faces to make sure everybody got the message that I was not the one to be played with this morning. "So get busy doing what you're being paid to do."

"Tate Alexandra!"

Mom. I rolled my eyes skyward.

"You don't have to be so abrupt, dear," she said, joining the impromptu gathering. "Good morning, gentlemen."

"Morning, ma'am." Joe nodded.

One of the guy's from the pick-up scrunched up his face in confusion. "*Abrupt?*"

"That's northern for *rude*," Joe replied with a glance in my direction.

I cleared my throat. "Unless Snappy Movers is giving out a special sarcasm discount today, get to work."

Joe and his crew gave me the stink eye before retreating to the back of the rig to get started. I looked over at mom who was still frowning. She opened her mouth to start in on me, but I beat her to the punch.

"Mom, I'm adulting here. Seeing as though you're the one who taught me to put on my big girl panties and handle my business, I'd appreciate it if you didn't scold me for doing just that."

I can feel your judgment again, trying to decide if you like me or not. It's easy to think *Alex should be nicer* when you're sitting on your fanny with a book in your hand. Right now, I don't have the luxury of being pleasant.

A deep sigh came from my mother's open mouth before she promptly closed it. Good. Now that everyone had been properly checked, we could focus on getting the furniture and boxes the movers had started unloading from the truck into my house.

I took a box marked 'kitchen' from one of the crew and started back up the bungalow's driveway. Movement from the house next door caught my eye, and I glanced up as a breeze rustled the curtains of an open window. My thoughts automatically drifted to my heated encounter with the house's owner two weeks ago.

"...that angelic face of yours won't stop me from getting down and dirty."

Taken out of context, a vow like that coming from a man who looked like Justice Lawson brought visions of rumpled sheets, sweat-slicked nude bodies and a blown out back to mind.

I quickly turned away and my gaze connected with the wizened faced of a garden gnome situated on my front lawn where the grass met a row of shrubbery. I blinked. I could have sworn the little statue wore a whimsical smile the first time I'd seen it. Now the damn thing looked eerily like the uncle I'd been named for. It also looked like it knew exactly what rabbit hole my mind had gone down and didn't like it one bit.

"Family first." My late great, great uncle's admonishment echoed in my head as the pissed off gnome glared at me. *"Don't you forget it, young Bridges, or I'll find my way back from wherever I am to remind you."*

Goosebumps erupted on my arms.

"You okay, hon?" My mother asked.

Shaking off my late uncle's ridiculous promise to haunt me from the grave, I assured her I was fine. If I'd admitted what I'd been thinking, she'd have just cause to put me in the lunatic category.

I gave the gnome a parting glance as I stepped onto my porch. The only thing Justice Lawson could do for me was move out of the house next door.

An hour later, I was using the power drill to reassemble my bed frame. It was part of the moving crew's duties, but I wanted to shave some time off their stay here as well as money off the final bill for their services. The dining room furniture had already been unloaded. Thank goodness Mom was here. While I was busy with the bedroom, she was instructing the moving crew on where to place my living room pieces. It would take the both of us to supervise the unloading and set up.

Only, once the whir of the drill stopped, the house was eerily silent.

No voices or clomp of the moving crew's heavy work boots against the hardwood floors. I put the drill down and walked to the living room, where it appeared a chair and half of my sectional had been unceremoniously dumped in the middle of the room.

What the—?

I went to the picture window. The flat screen television that I hadn't managed to unload on Craigslist sat abandoned on my driveway. My love seat and one of the large pieces that made up my entertainment center stood alone by the moving van. The moving crew and my mother were nowhere in sight.

I didn't know where they were or what was going on, but I intended to find out. One step out of my open front door and it hit me – an aroma that if I didn't know better would have convinced me I'd died and gone to heaven. I sucked in a deep breath of the sticky sweet air, while my nose discerned the scents of honey, sugar, fried chicken and sweet potatoes.

An unearthly growl sounded from my empty belly that made the ones coming from Joe's stomach earlier seem tame. Closing my eyes briefly, I inhaled again. Then my gaze followed the scent and sounds of laughter to the only other house on the street.

Lawson.

Crossing my driveway and stomping on Lawson's lawn, I kicked at a shingle that might have been ripped away from his roof in last night's storm. I charged up the porch stairs and knocked on the front door. Actually, I beat on it like it owed me money. No answer. I knocked harder. Guess no one heard me on account of all the muffled laughter coming from the back of his house. So I stomped around to the back. The delectable smells grew stronger with every step, so did the rumble of conversation and my disloyal mother's laughter.

It was obvious Mom and the moving crew were inside having a grand time with my enemy. Meanwhile, I stood on Lawson's back porch drooling, stomach growling, and mad as hell. I proceeded to give his back door the same pounding I'd given the front one. Too bad I couldn't kick it in.

I'd raised my fist to knock again when the door swung open and Justice Lawson filled the frame looking even better than I remembered. My breath caught in my throat as we stared at each other, and for a brief moment it appeared my unwanted attraction to him was mutual. But what do I know? I'm the same woman that entertained the idea that the gnome guarding my front lawn had been a reincarnate of my dead uncle.

"*Alexandra,*" Lawson drawled slowly, melodiously, as if my name was the refrain to a love song. He walked out the door onto the back porch. "I'd invite you to join us for breakfast, but it appears my unexpected company ate every bite." His already deep voice dropped an octave, and the dark eyes I'd thought had been mesmerized at the sight of me narrowed. "So you're shit outta luck, Bridges."

And just like that, I no longer saw tall, dark and handsome. All I saw was a Lawson. "You low down, dirty snake," I hissed, managing to sound just like one. "I wouldn't eat a peanut in the shell from this outhouse." I jerked my head in the direction of a bungalow that, except for being painted a putrid shade of green, looked exactly like the one I'd inherited, then jabbed a finger at it. "But that's *my* work crew in there, and they charge by the hour."

A smile spread over his lips, revealing even white teeth. "I may have overheard that fact."

I sucked in a deep breath to calm myself. Big mistake. The remnant of their breakfast assaulted my nose, and my stomach unleashed another unholy growl.

Lawson's dark eyes twinkled as he glanced down at my midsection. "Like I said Bridges, *shit outta luck.*"

I pushed past him through the door and into his kitchen. Technically, I was trespassing, but I had three workers and a disloyal mother to retrieve. The four of them were gathered around a kitchen table raving about the best breakfast they'd ever had over what appeared to be a second round of coffee.

"I've had chicken and waffles plenty of times," Joe said. "But never with sweet potato waffles. Delicious."

My mother raised her hand to her mouth to stifle a delicate burp. "And those biscuits with the homemade peach preserves! I lost count of how many I ate."

"Don't feel bad, ma'am. I made a total pig of myself." A guy from the moving crew chimed in. "I could use a good nap right now."

Nap! That did it. I cleared my throat loudly. They'd been so busy raving about their stupid breakfast no one had noticed I was even in the room. I leveled Joe and the work crew with my steeliest glare. "I'm not paying you three to fill your bellies and sit around yapping," I said. "Or maybe I should whip out my phone and upload a video of Snappy Mover's workers on the job to Instagram and Twitter."

Mom exhaled a long disapproving sigh. I ignored it.

"Uh, sorry, Miss," Joe said, sheepishly, as he slowly got to his feet. "Your neighbor here was kind enough to offer us a bite to..."

I held up a hand. "I don't want to hear it. All I want to see is the three of you doing your jobs."

Joe and the two workers shuffled past me mumbling more apologies. My gaze shifted to my mother. I'd told her all about the threats Lawson had made at the law office. *How could she?*

"Biscuits, honey," she said, as if I'd asked the question aloud. "And Applewood-smoked bacon with brown sugar." She glanced down at her empty plate. I wouldn't be surprised if she'd licked it. Then she turned to her host. "Did you make those peach preserves too?"

"Unfortunately, I can't take credit for the preserves. My late grandmother made them," Lawson said.

"Well, I certainly hope she left you the recipe," Mom said.

"She did." My neighbor nodded. "I haven't checked, but I'm also hoping she stashed a few jars out back in that old, underground storm cellar." He inclined his head toward the backyard.

Mom smiled up at him. "Don't tempt me to go out there and check," she joked.

I rolled my eyes and sucked my teeth, but both she and my neighbor seem oblivious.

"So glad you could join me for breakfast." Lawson's deep voice oozed Southern gentleman charm as he spoke to my mother. "Come back anytime, *Deb*."

"Deb!" I barked, and then turned to glare at my nemesis. How dare he act so familiar with *my mother?*

Pushing away from the breakfast table, Mom giggled like a smitten teenager. "It was delicious, Justice. You should open a restaurant."

"That's the plan, Deb." Lawson's face twinkled with amusement as if he knew using Mom's first name just twisted the knife that he was probably itching to bury in my back. "But first I have to handle a *hitch* with the financing."

"Is that a threat?" I asked, knowing my presence next door was the hitch he referred to.

Lawson didn't answer my question. No need. His new best friend, *Deb*, came to the rescue. "He did no such thing." Mom shook her head. "Don't be so dramatic, hon."

While my mouth's hanging wide open in shock, I might as well ask you if there's such a thing as loyalty pills? If so, pick up a bottle from Walgreens for my mother, *ASAP*.

"Yeah, don't be such a drama queen, Bridges," Lawson chimed in.

And while there's probably no need to tell you, the man's expression made it clear he was enjoying this.

I knew what he wanted. He'd love it if I showed out,

while he stood there looking innocent. I wouldn't give him the satisfaction, at least, not in front of my mother.

"Mom," I said as sweetly as I could manage. "I really need your help over at the house."

My mother blinked. "Oh, of course. I'd forgotten all about that." She smiled up at Lawson. "Those biscuits made me lose my head, and those sweet potato waffles! It was all so..."

"We all know breakfast was great," I interrupted, cutting my eyes in the direction of my house.

Catching the hint, Mom started for the door, but paused to break me off some unsolicited and frankly, stupid, advice. "I can tell you're annoyed," she said in a hushed whisper everyone could hear. "But a man who cooks like Justice can't be as bad as you say. He's also very easy to look at." She cast a quick glance in his direction, and then leaned to whisper in my ear. "That money is a long shot at best, but that man is son-in-law material. So be nice!"

Hold up. Forget what I said about Walgreens earlier. I'm gonna need you to head straight to Sam's Club for the supersize bottle of loyalty pills. On second thought, forget the pills. There's no hope for a mother willing to pimp out her only daughter for biscuits and bacon.

After mom cleared out, I turned to my neighbor. "I don't know what you were playing at plying the movers and my mother with food," I said. "You may have gotten in my mom's head with this act, but not mine. I'm not going anywhere. The only person leaving this street is you."

The screen door slammed against the back of his house as I shoved it and stepped onto the back porch. Lawson's footsteps and deep chuckle indicated he was right behind me.

"Hey, Bridges," he called out.

I stopped and spun around.

"It's not your head, I was out to get into," he said. "The thing with houses being so close together, when the windows are open, you can hear everything. After your movers casually mentioned they worked by the hour, I decided to get in your pocket."

He inclined his head toward my house. Mom was nowhere in sight. However, Joe and his two-man crew were still ambling toward my yard. They should have already been at the truck unloading. If I didn't know better, I'd think I was watching a movie filmed in slow motion.

What the hell?

Lawson stopped laughing long enough to answer my unspoken question. "You're looking at three severe cases of what's known in these parts as *the itis*."

"The what?"

"*The itis*," he repeated.

Whatever '*the itis*' was laughing like an idiot must be one of the symptoms, because Lawson's annoying ass couldn't stop.

"It's the drowsy condition folks contract after stuffing themselves with a huge meal. Mostly experienced on Thanksgiving after dinner," my neighbor explained.

I looked at the three men still lumbering toward my

yard. A sigh escaped from between my pursed lips as one of them stretched his arms over his head and yawned.

"Don't worry. All they need are strong naps, and they'll be as good as new." Lawson laughed again. "The way they're moving, I'd say I turned a three hour job into a six hour one easily."

"Come on, guys, get back to work," I yelled aloud, already planning to locate and unpack my coffeepot as soon as possible and counteract the effects of that damned *itis* with mugs of black coffee.

"You're wasting your time, lady, cause right now, your movers aren't worth a damn." Lawson stroked the layer of beard hugging his jawline. "But I'll tell you what, I'll pay for them to place what they've already unloaded back on that moving van. You can go back wherever you came from and forget your crazy uncle and that house next door ever existed."

This time I was the one laughing. "You'd like that, wouldn't you?" I asked. "*But I'll tell you what*, I'll cover the cost of them moving you out."

He shook his head. "Not going to happen."

I stepped up to him. "Then I suggest you watch your back, Lawson, because payback is a bitch and it's coming."

"So I've been told," he said, wearing the same smug smirk. "In the meantime, I'll tell you the same thing your old coot of an uncle once told me."

I crossed my arms over my chest. "And what's that?"

His smile vanished. "*Getcha ass off my porch, Bridges, before I get my shotgun.*"

5

"Never turn your back on a rattlesnake or a Bridges."

JUSTICE

FIRST OF ALL, I don't own a shotgun, but here's the deal.

I'd overheard the fellas moving Alex Bridges furniture griping about being starved, and then one of them mentioned that the woman paying them was on a tight budget and riding them to get the job done fast. Well, I'll tell you my original plan to greet my new, and as far as I was concerned, *very temporary neighbor* went out the same open window the movers conversation had floated through.

A new idea had popped into my head. Charming my neighbor's mother had been a bonus. After all, my beef wasn't with Deb. She was good people, and more importantly, she wasn't a Bridges.

If looks could kill, the daggers Alex had shot from those light brown eyes would have left me toes up at the church two streets over while a preacher officiated my send off.

Oh yeah, Bridges had been pissed.

My opening salvo to let my neighbor know just what she was getting into *should* have been perfect. Only I'd underestimated how attractive I found her and my reaction, specifically my dick's reaction. I guess this is my round about way of telling you that I chased her off my back porch with that shotgun threat before she caught sight of just how excited I was to see her.

That was yesterday.

Today was a new day. Yawning, I switched on the coffeemaker. No experimenting with breakfast recipes had canceled my morning visits from Ned. So I'd grab the newspaper from the front porch myself and skim the headlines while I figured out my next move to send that Bridges woman back to where she came from. Barefoot and clad in pajama bottoms, I stepped out on the front porch. Sunshine and the sound of birds chirping in the nearby trees greeted me, but the newspaper I'm sure I'd heard landing on my porch this morning wasn't there.

"Howdy, neighbor."

I turned to the sound of the voice to see Alex kicked back in the wicker chair old man Bridges used to sit in. Actually, all I really saw were legs, long shapely ones, propped up on the ledge of the porch railing and crossed at the ankles. My gaze trailed the length of them up to a pair of cut-off denim shorts that were frayed at the tops of her thighs.

Have mercy.

A bead of sweat broke out on my temple, and I licked my suddenly dry lips. Get it together man. The woman attached to those legs is the reason you aren't in NYC right now securing premises for your restaurant.

"I believe you have something that belongs to me," I called across the yard.

She peered at me over the top of the newspaper I knew she'd only pretended to read. "Really?"

"My paper."

My grandmother had insisted on home delivery, and I'd kept up the subscription. Grandma had considered both the online version of the paper and television news garbage. The former was riddled with too many pop-up ads for her taste, and the twenty-four hour news cycle had turned the latter into a bunch of shouting heads trying to tell folks what to think.

Like on so many other things, my grandmother had been right. I know what you're thinking, and I don't need you to tell me that if Grandma were here right now, she'd smack me upside the head for drooling over a Bridges.

My neighbor let the newspaper drop, revealing that freckled-face and hair that was more kinks than curls. She glanced down at the paper, before glaring across the yard at me. Our houses were close enough that I could see the smirk on her lips. "Don't see your name on it," she said.

Moving away from my front door, I walked to the side of my porch closest to her house and braced my palms against the railing ledge. "I'll bet Lawson is on the bag it came in." I shifted my eyes to the plastic sleeve next to her. "So what if I came over there and retrieved my property?"

Alex raised a brow, and her eyes narrowed. "Then I'd have to go inside for my uncle's shotgun and order you to *getcha ass off my porch.*"

Laughter bubbled up from my chest at her serving up the line I'd tossed out at her less than twenty-four hours ago. My ex used to make me laugh like that, but it seemed like a lifetime ago. Back then I was a sucker for a woman with a quick wit.

"Touché," I chuckled, not entirely sure she was joking. When old man Bridges had fired off those words, he'd been as serious as the heart attack that eventually killed him.

Alex lifted the paper, and once again, acted as if she were reading. Moments later she rested it on her lap with a sigh. "Don't you have anything better to do than gawk over here? Like go to a job?"

Shifting positions, I propped a hip on the ledge where my hands had rested. "Work nights, bartending at a sports bar, which leaves my days free to figure out how to get rid of you. In fact, I stepped out here to get my paper so I could peruse it while I strategized."

A snort erupted from across the yard, drawing my attention to her hot pink tinted pout. "Well, you're going to have to do better than that stunt you pulled yesterday, *way better*."

"Don't worry. I've got better."

"Keep in mind, I have the same motivation to get rid of you, Lawson," she said. "So don't get got. In fact, I'd suggest you sleep with one eye open."

"Or what? You'll steal my newspaper?" I shook my head. "You're going to have to do better than that, Bridges, *way better*. And for the record, I slept like a baby last night."

She rolled those light brown eyes and sucked her teeth. "I know. I heard your snoring through my bedroom window."

Thanks to the air conditioning being hit or miss, most of the windows at my place were open. The repairman said my central air unit needed to be replaced. *No shit.* However, new units came with a seven thousand dollar minimum price tag, and it wasn't something I wanted to invest in right now.

"Your bulldozer snores shook my house so hard, I thought it was thunder," Alex cracked. "I had to turn on the weather report to see if we were under a tornado watch."

I glanced across the street at the empty field where a row of houses once stood. "If there was a tornado around here, you'd know it, Bridges. What do you think wiped out the rest of the houses on this block? Any attempts at rebuilding met the same fate."

My neighbor's eyes widened, then narrowed with

suspicion. "And you're going to have to do better than trying to scare me too, Lawson."

I held off on divulging more of the street's history. She wouldn't believe it anyway. Doubt she even noticed both of our houses had lost some shingles or the fact there was an old underground storm cellar in my backyard.

Alex stood, and I noticed those endless legs were covered in the same freckles that kissed her face. "Unlike you, I don't have all day to stand around yapping. I have a job interview this morning." The smirk returned to her lips. "Put down some roots in my new community and all that."

"I would wish you luck, *but I don't.*"

"You're the one that's going to need luck, Lawson." She grunted. "This gig is only part-time. My full-time job will be running you out of that house so I can collect my dough." My neighbor rolled her eyes, before she went inside her house with my paper, slamming the front door behind her.

I had a list of chores to get to today, starting with mowing the lawn. Instead, I stood there staring at the chair she'd vacated grinning like an idiot.

Damn.

You caught me grinning about that little tête-à-tête, and now you're jumping to conclusions.

Mmm, hmm. You're not only attracted to Alex, you like her too.

Well, you couldn't be more wrong. Doesn't matter anyway because Alex Bridges days of occupying that house next door were numbered.

6

---

*"The grass isn't greener on the other side.
It's just fertilized with Lawson bullshit."*

ALEX

I'LL ADMIT SWIPING Lawson's newspaper was lame.

It didn't come close to the big payback I'd promised.
Still, I'd figured it would have to do until I could come up
with something better. You know, screw with his head a
little and let him know that infecting my movers with '*the
itis*' stunt wouldn't go unanswered.

But I wasn't ready.

I wasn't ready for him to step out of his door shirtless.
I wasn't ready for the sun to hit those broad shoulders

and bare chest at just the right angle making his torso resemble the sculpted bronzed statues admired in museums. I wasn't ready for the six-pack abs that made me want to explore each well-muscled ridge with my fingertips, then with my tongue.

And I damn sure wasn't ready for the snappy banter between us to be as addictive as looking at him.

The D.J. for the morning show I'd tuned in on my shower radio announced the time.

Shit!

Thanks to my screwing around taunting Lawson, I had less than an hour to get to my job interview. I shut off the *intentionally* cold shower, wrapped myself in a towel and began pulling myself together.

My mother had taken a late flight back to Chicago last night, and the house was still a mess. Fortunately, I'd located and unpacked my black suit last night before bed. Coming from NYC, there wasn't much in my wardrobe that wasn't black. I'd matched my go-to interview suit with a black and white floral shell top. Though the combination hadn't helped me land another position in advertising in the months since I'd left my old job, I'd hoped to snag a last minute opening at the local community college. The job was in their continuing education department, teaching evening classes focused on showing home-based entrepreneurs how to market their businesses.

The roar of a lawnmower drowned out the morning radio chatter. Standing at the bathroom mirror, I added a coat of mascara to my lashes and swiped on the bold power red lipstick I used to wear to work. Then I caught sight of my hair.

Dammit!

Fortunately, it was still wet, so I grabbed the tube of clear hair gel I'd forgotten in my rush. I squeezed a dollop into my palm and quickly scrunched it through my zigzag kinks to hold them in place. With no time to waste, I stepped into my black pumps, grabbed my purse and dashed out the door, car keys in hand.

I heard the lawnmower behind me as I walked briskly in the direction of my car, parked in the driveway.

Don't turn around, I told myself. Don't give Lawson a chance to get in your head before your interview and throw you off your game. Most of the time that warning voice in your head is right, but on this occasion, mine was dead wrong.

I felt it first, a tickle at my ankles and then the back of my legs.

Oh, no!

I spun around just as my neighbor mowed past me, his lawnmower spewing grass clippings all over me like confetti when the ball dropped on New Years Eve in Times Square.

"Lawson!" I bellowed over the mower's racket and glanced down at my once pristine, black suit, now covered in grass cuttings and tiny clumps of dirt.

Clad in jeans and a t-shirt, my neighbor's big body shook visibly, and when he turned to face me, his lips were pressed together trying to hold in a laugh. He looked me up and down before he spoke. "That your interview outfit?"

"Y-you know damn well it is," I sputtered, pausing to spit blades of grass from my mouth.

Lawson shrugged. (You read right, he freaking shrugged!) "So what's the job, mortician's assistant?"

"You suck!" I spit out more grass.

He jerked his head toward my house and raised a brow. "So move out."

"I don't have time for this." I also didn't have time to go back inside to change. So I brushed away the grass and debris best I could before yanking my car door open.

My neighbor called out to me as I slid behind the wheel. "Good luck!" He laughed. *"Not."*

Twenty minutes later, I pulled into the college's visitors' parking lot still fuming and calling Justice Lawson everything but a child of God. How could somebody so sexy, be so damn obnoxious?

Okay, I hear ya. For the same reason I'm trying to stomp on his last nerve, *money*. But like I said earlier, I don't have time to sit around navel gazing.

I jumped out of the car and swiped my hands over my clothes again. It appeared I'd wiped away most of the grass. There were some dirt smudges, but thanks to the black suit one would have to look hard to notice them.

Glancing at my phone, I checked the time and walked briskly toward a campus map.

"Ouch!" I yelped after a few steps, and then stopped

in my tracks. Standing on one leg, I slipped off my pump and shook it. More grass, dirt and a few pebbles fell onto the pavement. "Stupid, Lawson," I muttered.

I was shaking the same crap out of my other shoe when a security guard driving a golf cart pulled up beside me and stared open-mouthed. What was his problem? Hadn't he ever seen a woman stop to shake debris from her shoe?

"Everything okay, ma'am?" The guard asked, still gawking as if he were trying to decide if he needed to call for backup.

"Fine," I said, then explained where I needed to be for my interview and that I was short on time.

The dirt on my suit must have been more noticeable than I thought because he continued to just sit there and stare at me. "A job interview?" He pushed back his uniform cap and scratched his head. "You sure?"

I rolled my eyes in exasperation. "Yes, for a teaching position."

"Um...eh...well, hop on, I'll take you."

He dropped me off at the front of a building it would have taken me ten minutes to get to on foot. "The office you're looking for is on the second floor," the guard said, still looking at me strangely. "Uh...there's a ladies room near the stairwell if you want to...um...freshen up."

Again, I hadn't thought the grass stains and dirt smudges were as bad as all that. Even so, after running up the staircases leading to the second floor, I ducked into the ladies room to double check my outfit. I took one look in the mirror, opened my mouth and let out a silent scream.

Oh. My. Gawd.

Grass clippings covered my entire head. No wonder the security guard couldn't stop gawking at me, I looked like a Chia Pet. I shook my head, *hard*, to get rid of the grass and took another look in the mirror, but my 'fro remained completely covered in green.

I touched a tentative hand to my head and tugged at a blade of grass. It didn't budge.

"Shit!" I hissed. The memory of scrunching a handful of extra-hold styling gel through my hair before running out to the car replayed in my mind. The grass was good and stuck.

Justice Lawson had officially crossed the line. Didn't he know about the rule not to touch a sistah's hair. It was written on enough natural girls t-shirts. Okay, so he didn't exactly *touch* my hair, but he'd certainly fucked it up, and somehow, some way, I was going to make him pay.

Still staring at the mirror, I shook my head at my reflection. My grass helmet remained firmly in place. I sucked in a deep breath and slowly released it. Who would hire someone who walked into an interview looking like this? If my mom could see me now, I have no doubt she'd relegate me to that category she reserved for my father's family, *lunatics*.

I wanted to turn tail and go home.

My bank account vetoed that notion. I needed this job interview. I needed this job.

Squaring my shoulders, I reminded myself the

woman staring back at me in the mirror had come up with advertising campaigns that convinced millions of people to buy crap they didn't need. Now I was going to march into that interview and sell myself – grass green hair and all.

7

"A pretty face, thick thighs and a smile are dangerous, especially when they belong to a Bridges."

JUSTICE

THE NEXT MORNING, I stuck my head outside my front door first and looked both ways. Then I looked down.

No flaming bag of dog poop. No newspaper either.

Coffee mug in hand, I tentatively stepped onto the porch. Then I gave myself a mental shake. It wasn't like my neighbor had rigged it to explode. *Right?* But you know as well as I do when you mess with a black woman's hair – all bets are off, and so I'm sure once she caught sight of herself in the mirror yesterday, I held down the number one position on Alex Bridges' shit list.

My gaze traveled next door, where it connected with my newspaper, cut-off shorts and that incredible pair of freckled legs. Excuse me, but I need to pause right here, while my eyes roam from ankles to calves to thighs and back again to ask you a question: *how could anyone related to old man Bridges be blessed with legs like those?* I was imagining kinky scenarios with them wrapped around my waist when the newspaper covering her face fell to her lap.

My jaw dropped at the sight of the multi-colored turban covering her hair. Well, if she still had hair.

A little grass wouldn't make someone go bald, would it?

"You plan on saying good morning or just stand there gawking?"

"Uh...eh..." I stammered. The combination of the turban and her cool demeanor had thrown me.

Alex lifted a mug from the arm of her wicker chair and hoisted it in mock salute. "Early mornings are sacred. A bit of peace before I take the day on," she said. "So you can relax, *for now.*"

Continuing to stare at the turban, I unconsciously rubbed a hand over my own shaved head. Alex's gaze flicked upward and realization dawned.

"Deep conditioning my hair," she said, matter-of-factly. "It needed some TLC after that stunt you pulled."

The ingrained gentleman, that my neighbor hadn't seen much of, opened his mouth to apologize. Then I remembered my goal and whom I was talking to and promptly shut my trap.

"So did you end up going to that interview?" Now that I'd been assured her hair was intact, I was itching for details on what happened after she'd left yesterday.

Alex took a sip of her coffee, eyeing me over the rim of the mug. "I got the job," she said finally.

"Huh?" I blurted out. "But when you left here you were..."

She finished my sentence. "A mess."

"So how did you..."

This time, she finished my question. "Pull it off?"

Dumbstruck, I nodded.

"Because I'm good at what I do, Lawson." Defiance laced both her gaze and her tone.

Now I was really curious. Moreover, I was impressed. "And what exactly is it that you do?

"Advertising," she said. "Have you seen the commercial for the mobile phone where the outer space alien calls his mom on Mother's Day from Mars?"

I nodded. *Who hadn't?* Grandma had bawled every time it had come on.

"That was my campaign," Alex said. She proceeded to rattle off a few more products and their very catchy commercials.

Wow. Not only had I heard of the products, I'd been swayed by the commercials to buy many of them.

"So the community college's continuing education department was more than happy to have me teach four nights a week," she said. "The chairman of the department didn't mind that my hair looked like his front lawn. In fact, he praised my creativity."

Damn.

The woman not only had a sense of humor. She had to compound it by being smart. That was going to make her harder to get rid of. It was also getting increasingly difficult not to like Alex, a lot.

Uh, oh. You've got it all wrong. Now I need a brief interlude to set you straight. Stop imagining happily-ever-after scenarios involving my neighbor and me. This is a feud, and the only thing I'm walking away with, at the end of this tale, is a check for two hundred and fifty thousand dollars tucked in my back pocket.

Good. Now that we're on the same page, I can get back on task.

Propping a hip on the ledge of my porch railing, I sipped from my coffee mug. "Must have been hard for your former job to let you go," I said. "I'm willing to bet whatever they offered you to stay is a lot better than an old house and the promise of money that you're never going to get."

My neighbor's full lips pressed into a thin line. I'd definitely annoyed her – even more than I usually did.

"Then you'd be wrong, Lawson." Her jaw was clenched, and it looked like it hurt for her to push the words out of her mouth. "Three months ago, I walked into the executive offices of my agency expecting the promotion, corner office and partnership I'd worked my ass off to get."

I raised a brow. "And you didn't?"

She rested her mug on the arm of the wicker chair. "Nope. I stood there while they handed my partnership to a co-worker, a kid fresh out of college who'd only been at the agency six-months. Doubt the ink had dried on his degree," she said. "Oh, I should probably mention, that kid was the son of one of the agency's owners. Nepotism in action."

I sucked in a breath and exhaled it in a low whistle. Couldn't blame her for being pissed. Still, there had to be more to the story. What I'd heard so far didn't make good business sense, and I told her so.

"Oh, they offered me both a bonus and a sizeable raise to continue at my job." Alex grunted. "Basically, be a well-paid stooge while their golden boy took credit for my ideas."

"And I'd be correct in assuming you turned them down?"

She nodded and the corner of her mouth ticked upwards into a half smile. "I'll tell ya, Lawson, it was spectacular. I unloaded on them and explained exactly which orifices they could stick their offer in."

I couldn't help chuckle. The woman definitely had my respect. "So how did that go over?"

"About as you'd expect." Alex shrugged. "I was fired. They summoned security to stand guard while I packed up my desk. Twenty minutes later I was standing on Madison Avenue holding a cardboard box filled with my personal possessions."

She went on to explain how telling off her boss, while damned satisfying, had made it nearly impossible to lock down a new job in an already tight market.

"My unexpectedly inheriting this house was right on

time," Alex said. "I needed a place to regroup that wasn't costing me thirty five hundred a month in rent."

A hip propped up on the ledge of the porch railing, I rested my back against my house and drained the mug of my now cold coffee. Alex had gotten a rotten deal. If she had been anyone else, I'd offer some words of support. But she wasn't someone else. She was a Bridges, and her mere presence was screwing everything up for me.

I cleared my throat. "So what was your plan for the fat chunk of money that I'm standing in the way of you inheriting?" I asked, and then speculated. "Go back to New York and continue to look for work? Get a job with your old agency's competition?" As talented as she was, I was sure she'd eventually get hired. Even with a lackluster reference from her former employer.

Alex folded the newspaper resting on her lap. "Initially, that was exactly my plan."

"And now?"

"I've had a little time to think about it, and I don't think I want another job," Alex said. "I don't want to work for my old job's competition either, *I want to be the competition.*"

"As in starting up your own agency?"

Alex nodded. "Mind you, I'm doing it regardless of if and when I run you out, but that inheritance money would go a long way in ramping up my timetable."

"You'll have to rely on your talent, lady, because I won't be leaving here until *after* you do."

"Don't count on it," she said.

Easing my hip off the ledge, I stood. Thanks to my

stupid curiosity, I knew too much. I wanted to look across the yard and simply see the enemy or as my grandma would say, 'one of those damned Bridges'. Now Alex was more than just a pretty face. She was a decent person who possessed the same dream of entrepreneurship that I had.

I nodded in her direction, before turning and walking toward my front door.

"Hold up," Alex called out. "Where do you think you're going?"

I turned around. "Inside. You haven't run me out of my house, yet."

Standing, Alex walked to the edge of her porch. "Oh, no you don't."

Call me slow, but I had no idea what she was talking about.

Alex shook her turban-swathed head and admonished me with a wave of her index finger. "I spilled my gut answering your nosy questions. Time for you to tell me your backstory."

"But I only asked about your work and what you would do if you ever got your hands on your family's feud clause money?"

Alex crossed her arms over her chest. "Sounds like a good place to start," she said. "My mom mentioned you're a Parisian-trained chef. So how come you're bartending instead of running a kitchen in a fancy restaurant?"

"It's a long story," I began, "but I...

Alex raised a hand. "Hold that thought. I'm going to need another cup of coffee." She grabbed her mug, but stopped when she reached her front door. "You got anything to eat over there?"

I was about to say no, and then I remembered the double-batch of cinnamon walnut muffins I'd made for Grandma's church league's annual tea. Although my grandmother was gone, the event had been dear to her heart, and when old church ladies ask a favor – I do it.

"Yeah, I may have a little something," I said. Also, more coffee did sound good.

When I returned minutes later, a second cup of coffee and two muffins in hand, my neighbor was sitting cross-legged in the wicker chair. A frown creased her pretty features, and if I didn't know better I'd think she was talking to the garden gnome positioned in front of her porch.

"You okay?" I asked.

Alex abruptly turned away from the yard statue. "Eh...I'm fine." Rising from the chair, she came to the edge of her porch. "So what's that in your hand?"

"Catch." I tossed one of the muffins across the yard, and she caught it with both hands.

Sigh. Couldn't you have just walked it over?

There you go with the judging again. Let me refresh your memory. This is a feud. We may be on speaking terms, but our last names haven't changed.

Alex sat on the ledge of the porch railing facing my house, then swung her legs around until they dangled off the side. I took what had become my usual position on my porch, when having a conversation with my neighbor, hip propped up on the railing and my back resting against the front of my house.

My neighbor sniffed the muffin. "You make this?"

I nodded.

"Well, let me see what you got."

Alex took a bite, and I awaited her reaction. Not that it mattered. It wasn't like I wanted to impress her.

Looks like you do.

Okay, so maybe I did a little. She was slowly chewing when I caught it – a soft moan escaped her lips as her eyes rolled back in her head, and an expression of pure bliss overtook her face.

Oh, yeah. She was impressed all right.

I swallowed hard. And I couldn't help fantasize about touching and tasting her in ways that would evoke that same expression, make her eyes roll back in her head as the breath that carried her soft moan fanned against my face.

Yeah, my mind went there. So what. I'm not some cardboard hero. I'm a grown assed man.

Alex polished off the oversized muffin in two bites, and I asked the question, although I already had my answer. "Good, huh?"

She smiled, a full-blown grin that lit up her entire face. It made me think of the way she'd smiled at me back at the lawyer's office before she'd caught my last name. Her gaze dropped to my hand, and she licked her lips. "You plan to eat that?"

I tossed my muffin across the short distance separating our porches. She caught it and took a huge bite.

"So you were about to explain your career moves? How did a marginally-talented chef end up working as a bartender?"

Raising a brow, I zeroed in on the muffin she was stuffing into her mouth. "Marginally talented, huh?" I laughed. "Just try not to chew your fingers off, Bridges."

Unbothered, Alex continued eating as I told her about returning to Nashville after my grandmother's cancer diagnosis. "I came back with a six-figure bank account, a job as sous chef at a restaurant outside of Paris, shoulder-length dreadlocks, and a fiancé."

Sometime between my explaining how I'd quit my job to care for grandma, spent my savings on life-extending drugs, and my fiancé dumping me, Alex stopped eating. Her coffee mug sat beside her on the ledge untouched as she stared at me.

I didn't just see the understanding in her face - *I felt it*. I felt her as if she'd crossed the property line and covered my hand with hers.

"A childhood friend gave me a job at his sports bar," I continued. "I'd worked my way through culinary school bartending so it was an easy fit. I worked evenings while home health care nurses looked after grandma."

Then I went on to explain what Alex really wanted to know, *why I was still here*. "After grandma died, I'd intended to sell the house, take a job in New York, re-build my savings and eventually open my own restaurant. Then her will was read."

"The feud clause," Alex said.

I nodded. "No way I'd leave and let your mean assed

uncle collect on your family's feud clause. Then he up and died, so I only had to wait six-months for the Lawson feud clause money to be turned over to me," I explained. "While I waited, I came up with a plan to open a breakfast-only café. I was going to use the inheritance money and borrow the rest from the bank."

Alex nodded. "But I showed up."

I stared down at my coffee mug. "Yup. From out of nowhere on the very last day."

A long beat of silence passed between us. When I looked across the yard to Alex's porch, I wondered if she was thinking the same thing. If the circumstances were different, if our last names weren't Bridges and Lawson...

I shook my head at the ridiculous notion.

"Your dreads?" Alex finally spoke. "You never said what happened to them."

I ran a hand over my scalp. "When my grandmother lost her hair to chemo, I shaved mine off in solidarity. A two cue balls are better than one thing." I shrugged. "Kept it shaved ever since."

Alex swallowed hard as if there was something lodged in her throat. "Just so you know, I'm sorry about your grandmother."

Shit. Her heartfelt reaction caught me off guard.

"Thanks," I acknowledged aloud, then uttered a reminder to both her and myself. "But if grandma were here today, she'd hate your Bridges's guts."

I caught Alex's smile before it vanished, but she couldn't hide the amusement in her eyes. "Rest assured, Lawson, the feeling would be entirely mutual."

8

"Revenge is beneath me, but when it comes to a Lawson –
shit happens."

ALEX

Just. Chill. Out.

I could barely focus on what Lawson was saying. All I could hear was you yapping in my ear.

"Girl, what's with all the smiling, I thought you were going to get that man back."

I am.

"You do remember what he did to your interview outfit, right? Your hair? Not to mention, he rendered your moving crew useless by stuffing them like Thanksgiving turkeys."

I remember.

"All I saw was you on the brink of bawling over his sob story and getting yourself sprung."

Maybe. But that won't stop me from doing what I have to do.

"Do? Hunny, I don't know what had you drooling more, the muffins or the stud muffin?"

Whatever. You know as well as I do Justice Lawson is the total package. It wasn't enough for him to be fine as hell. *Noooooo.* He had to go and make it worse by being selfless, compassionate, ambitious, and an incredibly decent human being.

Hmm, mmm. Nose wide open.

Regardless, I fully intend on paying Justice Lawson back.

"So exactly when are you going to do it, huh?"

Ahem. This is *my* story. Don't be so damn bloodthirsty. And for goodness sake, have a little patience. The man shaved his head for his dying grandma, who wouldn't get all up in their feelings over that?

"Hey! One last question, were you really talking to that garden gnome that looks like your late great, great uncle?"

Uh...um...of course not. That would make me a lunatic.

9

"Sometimes you get one over on a Bridges.
Sometimes the Bridges gets one over on you."

JUSTICE

THE SHINGLES on my roof weren't going to replace themselves, and I'd put it off long enough.

If you're wondering how a chef learned how to repair a roof – YouTube. Thanks to their online videos I could handle most repairs around the house and even a few on my car.

But that's not what you're wondering, is it? Nah. You're wondering where my head is after this morning's encounter with my neighbor. You want to know if I'm catching feelings.

None of your damned business.

Sounds like you're protesting a bit too much.

Probably. And if circumstances were different, I might have spent the remainder of the morning filling a wicker basket with special delicacies, and then grabbed a bottle of wine, a blanket and asked my neighbor out for an afternoon picnic. Explore our attraction. Get to know her better. But feelings aren't facts, and the circumstances between Alex and I aren't going to change.

So instead, I spent the rest of the morning walking up and down the aisles at Home Depot filling an orange cart with roofing cement, roofing nails and asphalt shingles that were a close enough match to the aging roof of the house. When I returned home, I immediately began unloading my purchases. I'd climbed the ladder to survey the roof the other day and noticed most of the missing shingles were on the side of the house by my neighbor.

My gaze traveled to her porch as I dropped the bundle of shingles on my side of the property line. Alex's car was parked in the driveway, but there was no sign of her.

Good.

Today's task was about more than patching the roof before the rain predicted in the extended weather forecast made its appearance in a few days. I needed a mental reset and physical labor was just the trick to put things back in their proper perspective. By the time I finished the roof repairs, my only thoughts of Alex Bridges would be driving her pretty ass out of the house next door.

I finished unloading the supplies, and then walked

around to the other side of the house where I'd left the extension ladder. I should have put one on my Home Depot shopping list, I thought, as I rounded the house again and re-positioned the ladder.

Too late now.

Thanks to my wasting half the morning lusting over Alex Bridges and talking way too much it was already hot outside. If I stopped now to return to the big box hardware store, shop for a ladder, and then drive back home, the sun would be high in the sky and the roof would be sizzling.

It took three trips up and down the ladder to get the supplies on the roof. When I was done, I stood on the sloped roof, pushed back my Yankees cap and used my forearm to swipe at the sweat rolling down my face. I grabbed the bottle of cold water I'd brought up on the last trip and took a big gulp.

Time to fix my roof and my mindset.

I spared another glance at the house next door. I'd been running out of my house mornings acting like we had some kind of coffee date. No more. The next time I saw Alex Bridges, I was going to treat her like exactly what she was – someone standing in the way of my goals and a member of a family that had loathed mine for nearly a hundred years.

Donning work gloves, I used a flat bar to pry up what was left of a damaged shingle and remove the old nails. Next I slipped the new shingle in place, secured it with new nails and roof cement. The weather-beaten shingle that high winds had no problem ripping in half had required some muscle to remove. Otherwise, it had been simple enough. Just like on the YouTube videos I'd watched on repeat.

I stood to examine my work. Though I'd matched them best I could, the new shingle stood out making the roof look a bit like a patchwork quilt.

Still, not bad.

Okay, it looked like shit, but it would keep water from leaking down on my head, and unless you're in a plane flying overhead, you'd never know.

I took another swig from my water bottle. This sun wasn't playing, and there were plenty more shingles to replace. Pulling my phone from the back pocket of my jeans, I took off my glove and swiped the screen. Time to call in reinforcement.

Ned's voicemail kicked in.

"Hit me back when you get this message," I said, then swiped the screen to hang up.

I was slipping the phone into the chest pocket of my t-shirt, when I caught movement out the corner of my eye. At first, I thought the sun was playing tricks on me because it looked like the ladder was moving. I blinked.

Shit! It *was* moving.

I scrambled to the edge of the roof as fast as the steep slope would allow and looked down. Alex gripped the sides of the ladder, and it looked as if she were about to climb up.

"What in the hell are you doing on my side of the property line?" I bellowed. There was no time like the present to nip this attraction in the bud. My neighbor needed to know her company wasn't welcome in my yard or on my roof.

Squinting, Alex craned her neck to look up at me and smiled brightly. "Hello again, neighbor."

"Get off my damn property, Bridges," I ordered. For the record, I didn't enjoy being an asshole, but what choice did I have? You know our situation.

Alex's smile widened. Sigh. Why couldn't the woman be ugly like her uncle? "Actually, I'm only over here to retrieve *my property*," she yelled up at me.

Before I could grasp what she was saying, Alex walked away - *with the freaking ladder.*

"Hold up! Come back with that!" I lunged for the ladder and nearly fell off the roof. I managed to regain my balance, but my phone tumbled out of my pocket and dropped to the grass below. "Damn!"

Now on her side of the property line, my neighbor stopped in her tracks. Leaning the lightweight aluminum ladder against her house, she pointed to the chicken scratch written on the side of it. Even from the roof I could make out the words as she read aloud. *"Property of Tate Bridges."* Grinning, she jabbed her thumb in the direction of her chest. "That's me. Well, not exactly, but close enough."

I held up my hands in surrender. "Okay, I borrowed the ladder from your uncle's shed, before you came on the scene," I confessed. "I was wrong, and I apologize. Now if you'll just bring it back long enough for me to get down from here, I'll go buy my own."

Still looking up at me, Alex shook her head. "No can

do, Lawson."

"Yeah, you can. It'll only take me a few moments to climb down, then it's all yours."

She shook her head again. "Sorry. Can't cross the property line. That would be trespassing."

"But you were just over here a minute ago. You're over here every morning, swiping my newspaper." Taking off my cap briefly, I swiped at the sweat on my forehead. "Okay, I'm giving you permission to come on my property and bring that ladder."

"I'll pass."

Now the sweat rolling off me wasn't just from the heat. That ladder was the only way for me to get down from here without the high probability of breaking several bones, and I appeared to be shit out of luck on her letting me use it, even briefly.

"Well, can you at least grab my phone and try to throw it up here?"

"Nope."

I heaved an exasperated sigh. "Stop playing."

"Oh, this isn't playing." Alex was quick to correct me. "It's called payback, Lawson, and I warned you *she was a bitch.*

———

THE GOOD NEWS is I'd replaced all the damaged shingles. The bad news is that I finished the job over an hour ago, and I was past ready to get the hell off this hot assed roof.

Want to know what I've been doing to pass the time? Probably not, but since I'm currently stuck and have nothing better to do, I'll tell you anyway.

I worked. I paced. I threatened. I pleaded.

But that stubborn Bridges wouldn't budge. In fact, she'd gone back into her house a while ago claiming *she had shit to do.*

I sat on the edge of the roof near the front of my house with my feet hanging off the side. The drop was too long to jump. I'd only end up going from stuck on my roof to being stuck in a hospital bed. The gutter wasn't strong enough for me to attempt to shimmy down. My back porch was also too far of a drop from the roof to jump. That left me with two options. Hope that Ned would get my message and drop by or that my sole neighbor would take mercy on me.

Scratch that.

Those weren't options. They were long shots. In the meantime, I was baking like an Easter ham. Then I heard the sound of a door opening and closing coming from the back of the house next door. Standing, I walked along the edge of the roof in the direction of our backyards.

I looked down and staggered, nearly tumbling off the roof.

Don't panic. The unrelenting heat hadn't got to me. It was the sight of Alex Bridges reclining in a lawn chaise, clad in one of the sexiest bikini's I'd ever seen.

Have mercy. Not only was the bright orange shade of her swimwear my new favorite color - this roof just got a hell of a lot hotter.

Alex raised her sunglasses to her forehead and looked up at me. "Ah, you're still up there," she said.

You'd think a man in my position would have adopted a Keith Sweat from the 90s attitude and try to beg his way out of this. Nope. I had my pride - my stuck on a hot roof drooling over the enemy, can't let a Bridges beat me down - pride. "Where else would I be?" I asked.

Sliding her sunglasses back into place, Alex shrugged. "Thought you would have reached out to a friend for help."

"And just how am I supposed to call anyone with my phone on the ground?"

Even from my perch on the roof, that smile of hers was easy to spot. "Oh, yeah, that," she said.

"I don't suppose you've had time to think this through and come to your senses, maybe bring that ladder back or try tossing my phone up here?"

"Actually, all I've thought about is coming out here to soak up some of these rays. Don't want you hogging all this sun."

Hogging this sun? That did it! I shouted down a few curse words that I don't care to share with you. Yeah, they were even worse than the ones you've already come across.

Alex yawned and reached into a beach bag next to her chair, pulling out a book and a bottle of what appeared to be lemonade. Damn, I licked my dry lips. Lemonade would really hit the spot about now.

My bikini-clad neighbor hoisted the bottle in mock salute before taking a thirsty gulp. "I like my revenge like my lemonade, *served ice-cold."* She took another sip, rested the bottle on the arm of the chaise, and cracked open her book.

As pissed as I was over my current situation, I had to give Alex credit. Not only had she been savvy enough to seize an opportunity (and that ladder), she'd also known how to really rub it in. The move with the lemonade had been genius. If it were just about my pride and this stupid feud, I would have reconsidered my stance on begging.

I won't lie. I probably would have asked her out too. I mean, why did black women have to look so damn delicious in orange?

However, there was also a life-changing amount of money at stake, and it would take more than a hot roof and a smart woman with a hot body to make me forget it.

"So you're just going to kick back and read while I'm up here in the sweltering heat?" I asked finally.

Alex looked up. I was hoping she was finally about to take pity on me when a phone rang. She reached into the bag beside her and pulled out a phone.

"Hi, Mom," she said, answering it.

Mom. Deb adored me. I was confident she would either send help or convince that lowdown, stinkin' Bridges daughter of hers to do the right thing.

"Deb! Deb!" I called out.

"Uh...yes, Mom. That's Justice you hear in the background. Yes, we're playing nice." Alex spoke so sweetly I nearly got a cavity.

I stood and called out to her mother again.

"Has Justice been cooking?" Alex asked, apparently

repeating her mother's question. "Yes, ma'am. *He's cooking all right.*" She shot a look up at me on the roof and snickered.

Damn, Bridges.

"Help, Deb! Help me!" I shouted.

"Yes, Mom. That was Justice. He needs help in the kitchen." Alex scrambled up from the chaise and walked to the other side of her yard.

"Help! She's got me trapped on the roof," I yelled. "Call the ..."

"Yes, he needs my help right now. Bye, Mom!"

My shoulders slumped as I watched Alex saunter back to her chaise, a shit-eating grin on her face. She looked up at me. "Nice try, Lawson." She took a long gulp of lemonade and sank back into the chaise. "Now let's talk seriously about your moving out of that house of yours, so I can collect the rest of my inheritance."

I glared down at her. "This roof would have to combust into flames before that happened."

Shrugging, Alex picked up her book again. "Suit yourself."

Then I saw it.

I closed my eyes briefly to make sure it was for real and this sun didn't have me hallucinating. But it was still there and getting closer. Ned's car was coming down Old Trail Avenue. I nearly collapsed with relief as he turned into my driveway.

An ice-cold beer and a cold shower were first on my agenda. Then I'd figure out my Alex Bridges problem.

10

"When you're feuding with a Lawson - petty is as petty does."

ALEX

REVENGE WASN'T ALL THAT.

Don't get me wrong – it was sweet, and the look on Lawson's face when I pointed to my name on that ladder was priceless. I nearly peed my pants laughing.

Even so, payback wasn't nearly as satisfying as I'd expected it to be, especially considering the crap he'd pulled on me. And to be honest, it left me feeling like a piece of shit.

So why didn't you just put the ladder back, and let him get down from that hot roof?

Are you s-l-o-w? I'm embroiled in a feud here. Not to mention, there's a hell of a lot of money at stake. And please don't bother hitting me up with one of those bull-shit platitudes about money not being important. Ever try paying your rent or a cashier for a cart full of groceries with kindness, love, or happiness?

Didn't think so.

So after I'd snatched that ladder, I'd hidden inside my house where there was no chance I'd cave in to guilt or these unwanted feelings that had crept up on me for Justice Lawson. I'd opened my laptop and checked my dwindling bank balance. It had been just the reminder I'd needed to get my head straight.

I'd returned to the backyard determined to show him I could make being neighbors just as unpleasant for him as he'd tried to make it for me.

The bikini?

Oh, I'd worn it to even up the score. Every time, Lawson stepped out on his porch looking for his paper I squirmed in my underwear, and that morning he'd come out san shirt, *good gracious*. I just hoped the man didn't own a pair of gray sweatpants.

Hold up.

I'm not saying the sight of him in that particular garment would make me do something stupid like give up my shot at my family's feud clause money. However, depending on what he was packing I might be tempted to wave a white flag, constructed of my white lace panties, and broker a *temporary* dick truce. You know, hit it and forget it.

I feel your judgment, but I'm ignoring it. We're all adults here.

Anyway, back to explaining that totally unnecessary bikini. You'd have to be blind not to notice the way Lawson ogles my legs. So I reasoned, why not put something on his mind? If he was going to play a prominent role in my late night fantasies, I wanted to fuck up his sleep too.

What can I say? Legendary, hundred year old feuds have a way of bringing out the petty.

Still, if I was going to best Lawson, I had to stop thinking about sex every time I looked at him. Easier said than done. I contemplated solutions to my dick-on-the-brain dilemma as I walked to the kitchen to grab another bottle of lemonade from the fridge.

I started to call one of my girlfriends. The move to Nashville had cut me out of my weekly girls' night fix. I looked at the clock. They were all at work, and this was too much to explain in a text. So instead I asked myself, *what would I advise a friend in my situation to do?*

The solution was a no-brainer.

Get. Freaking. Laid.

After all, wasn't the best way to forget one man is to hook up with another one?

Unfortunately, I didn't know anyone here. So I went back to my laptop and looked up the online dating site a friend had found her husband on. No. I'm not looking for a husband. However, I began filling out the site's questionnaire with what I was looking for – tall, dark-skinned, bald, bearded....

Oh, why bother telling you what you already know?

11

"You can't do big things if you're distracted by a Bridges."

JUSTICE

"Old man Bridges' niece seemed nice enough to me."

Of course, Ned would believe that. The moment he'd stepped out of his car, I'd yelled from the roof for him to go buy an extension ladder – *ASAP*. Instead, my best friend had introduced himself to the enemy and then asked to use the very same ladder Alex had snatched away from my house.

Get this. My neighbor had pasted a smile on that pretty mug of hers, waved a hand in the direction of the ladder and told Ned that *he* was welcome to use it. Just like that. After she'd stranded me on my roof for hours.

Can you believe that shit?

Sigh. Why did I even ask? I should have known you'd throw that business with the movers and the grass-Afro incident back in my face. You can rest your case, because I don't want to hear about what *I* did. That's not the point. The point is what that lowdown, ornery Bridges did to me.

"And the woman doesn't look anything like her uncle." Pausing, Ned looked up from counting down the register. He'd taken pity on me after the roof situation and covered tonight's shift behind the bar.

However, I got sick of sitting around the house stewing about my neighbor, so I'd come in just before closing to catch the end of the Yankees game and get out of my own head. Only I couldn't concentrate on the game because all Ned could talk about was Alex Bridges.

"Did you see that orange bikini?" Ned asked. "I should say did you catch that body of hers in that orange bikini?" My friend blew out a low whistle. "I nearly dropped down on one knee and proposed."

I grunted from my seat on the other side of the bar.

Ned shook his head. "I don't know how you stay focused on that old feud with a woman that looks like her."

Abandoning the count, my friend offered me a beer, but I opted for a bottle of lemonade instead. I unscrewed the cap and took a thirsty gulp. "You mean the woman who spent most of the day torturing me?"

Ned snorted. "She can tie me up and torture me all night long."

"Excuse me while I try to scrub that image from my brain." I took another gulp of lemonade.

Don't come at me with a load of psychobabble bullshit about my suddenly drinking lemonade being subliminally tied to my neighbor. I just had a taste for it. That's it.

More like had a taste for Alex Bridges.

I heard that. Shut up. I'm trying to watch the game.

Ned grabbed himself a beer. I caught the shifty look on his face, and having known him all my life, I knew exactly what he was about to ask me.

"No."

"What do you mean, no?" My friend asked, incredulous. "I haven't even asked you anything."

"So ask."

Ned cleared his throat. "I was just going to run the idea of my asking your neighbor out for a..."

"No." I repeated, before he could even get the question out.

"Why not?"

"Because she's a Bridges."

A smirk overtook Ned's features before he took another pull from his beer. "Yep, just what I thought," he said, finally. "I could practically see the sparks flying off you two earlier today. That feud isn't the only thing going on between you and your neighbor."

I wanted to protest. Argue that the only thing my friend had seen earlier were the wisps of smoke coming off my sunbaked black ass. But Ned had also known me all his life. I drained the lemonade and rested the bottle on the bar. You would think roasting atop a hot roof for hours, basting in my own sweat would have been enough to squash my infatuation with Alex.

It hadn't.

Although, I'd thought about the feud, the money and my next move to push her out of that house next door, my dominant thoughts had been memories of Alex stretched out on her lawn chaise clad in that sexy orange bikini.

No. I didn't want to be tied up and tortured by her like my freak of a best friend, but I could bite, lick, and taste every freckle on Alex Bridges body, *over and over again.*

Ned aimed the remote at the television and turned it off.

"Hey, I was watching the game," I protested.

"Game's been off for ten minutes," he said. "Yankees lost."

I sucked in a deep breath and slowly released it. "How am I ever going to get my hands on my family's feud clause money if I can't get that woman out of my head?"

Ned raised his beer bottle, but paused before taking a sip. "Why don't you two just fuck each other's brains out and get it out of your systems?" He offered.

I frowned. Hadn't he heard a word I'd said? "Because she's the last woman I should be attracted to. I damn sure don't need to try to act on it."

Ned shrugged a shoulder. "Why not? She's grown. You're grown. It's obvious you both want it."

My friend made it sound simple. First of all, I wasn't

so sure Alex was as hot for me as I was for her. Not that I should even be entertaining the notion. Sex between her and me wasn't happening. "Because fucking can lead to feelings," I answered. "I don't want a relationship. I want Alex Bridges out of my head and out of that house next door."

My friend didn't miss a beat. "Then fuck somebody else."

His logic escaped me.

"And exactly how is that going to convince Alex to give up and move?"

"One problem at a time," Ned said. "Right now, you're trying to get her off your mind, right? And the best way to forget a woman is to screw another one. "

Did I mention the advice Ned loved to disburse was crap? However, this idea wasn't half bad. Also, it could be that I wasn't hung up on Alex Bridges after all. It had been a while. I just needed to get laid.

Ned jerked his head toward the tip jar at the other end of the bar, where women's business cards rested among the dollar bills. "It's not as if you don't get pussy practically thrown in your face every ladies night."

Retrieving the jar, he reached into it and withdrew a business card that had been slid across the bar to me the other night. The card was pink, so it stood out among the others, and I remembered the woman who'd scribbled her personal number on the back of it.

Ned read the card and raised a brow. "So the cutie with the pixie cut and curves is a yoga instructor."

"How do you know what she looked like? I could

have sworn you were back in the kitchen when she'd slipped it to me."

My friend shrugged. "While I was watching her, apparently she'd been watching you." Ned extended the card to me. "Now call the yogi and see if you can't get your head screwed on straight."

12
___

"Mistakes are proof that a Lawson has been working your nerves."

ALEX

7 PM – Walk into bougie French restaurant to meet my online date with high hopes. I'm wearing my do-me sling-backs and carrying a beaded clutch stuffed with condoms prepared to forget all about Justice Lawson.

7:04 pm –Walk out of restaurant after its revealed my date had uploaded a photo that was obviously taken forty years ago. While he was indeed dark-skinned (wrinkled), bald (as in male pattern) and bearded (think Santa), no way I believed the lie he'd just pushed out from between his top and bottom dentures.

Twenty-eight years old my ass.

13

"Thoughts of a Bridges are like roaches – hard to obliterate."

JUSTICE

The yoga instructor's name was Kiara.

When I called her, I still wasn't sure if asking her out was such a good idea. Then she met me in front of the restaurant – braless and wearing a cropped t-shirt and jeans that showcased a tiny waist that flared into hips a man could grip all night long.

Oh, yeah. Yoga definitely did a body good.

For the record, I'm well aware of your disapproval. It's not like I could miss the laser beam side eyes, grunts and the sucking of teeth. You're ready to brand me a dog, but before you do let me refresh your memory.

I'm not married.

I'm not engaged.

I'm not even seeing anyone.

Know what that makes me? The question's rhetorical, but I'll answer. It makes me a bachelor.

So I'm calling bullshit on your, *'Justice is a dog!'* allegations, and for the umpteenth time reminding you that I'm a grown assed man. Grown *single* men like hooking up with pretty women with hot bodies.

What about Alex?

Pardon me, but I didn't just sit across the table from Kiara at her favorite vegetarian restaurant tonight to think about Alex Bridges. *Sigh.* I'm here to forget about the fact that I practically race to my porch every day, because I know my neighbor will be sitting on hers, all boldly painted lips, freckles, and endless legs. I'm here to forget Alex's quick wit, tenacity and spirit. The bottom line is I'm trying like hell to rid myself of feelings for her that I don't want or even understand.

So get off my back about Alex, and knock it off with the grunts and teeth sucking. You've made your point. Now let me try to find something decent to eat off this damned meatless menu.

Kiara glanced up from her menu. "I've heard the buffalo cauliflower is good," she said. "My friends say it tastes exactly like the chicken version."

I highly doubted it, but didn't say so. "You haven't tried it for yourself?"

My date shook her head. "I don't eat vegetables."

Huh? Apparently I'd missed something. "But you said you didn't eat meat and this *vegetarian* restaurant was your favorite?"

"The pesticides in fruits and vegetables can be just as harmful as meat," she said.

"What about organic?" I asked, mildly curious as to what exactly she did eat.

"I'm sure you've heard of incidents of E. coli outbreaks in lettuce and even peanut butter," Kiara said.

Of course, but they were infrequent occurrences. I didn't argue though. I also didn't mention my background as a chef. The truth was I didn't want to get to know my date, I just wanted to get with her, if you catch my drift.

Kiara closed her menu and rested it on the table. "I only eat beans."

I stared at her a moment. "Beans? That's it?"

My date nodded. "You never hear about a recall or public health crisis over beans, do you?"

She had a point, still. "Even for breakfast?" I asked.

Kiara nodded again.

"Dessert?"

"Beans."

"That's a limited diet, isn't it?" Mind you, I was just making small talk. Didn't matter to me what she ate. It hadn't even occurred to me to fill a picnic hamper with gourmet delicacies, feed her and learn everything there was to know about her as I longed to do for Alex. Never mind. I'm not supposed to be thinking about my neighbor.

The waiter came to the table. I decided to give the buffalo cauliflower a shot and added a salad. Kiara selected a three-bean bowl.

"There are enough different kinds of beans in nature to provide me with plenty of variety," she said. "Beans are natural and incredibly healthy. They keep me looking good and feeling great.

"I see." To tell the truth it sounded kooky as hell, but to each his own. Besides, she did look good.

Kiara and I spent the next hour engaged in conversation and eating. The cauliflower was surprisingly tasty. The company wasn't half bad. Okay, so I'd only heard about half of what she'd said. That braless rack of hers kept diverting my attention. *Dayum!* Not only did it defy gravity, it appeared to do so without surgical enhancements.

Last reminder. Grown assed man.

My date's gaze met mine, before it fell to her chest. "Everything about me is natural and a hundred percent real," she said, as if she'd read my mind. The smile on her face indicated she was flattered and not at all offended.

It turned out Kiara was recently divorced, and now that she'd broken free of the shackles of matrimony (her term, not mine) she was eager to jump into the single life, *very eager*.

"I'm glad you called," she said "But to be honest, dinner and a movie weren't what I had in mind when I saw you behind the bar and slipped you my number."

"What exactly did you have in mind?" I asked, though I had an idea.

Kiara slid her tongue across her bottom lip in a way that made me wonder what else she was willing to do with that tongue tonight. I stared at her mouth awaiting an answer to my question. Instead, I felt a bare foot touch my crotch under the table.

"I don't want a relationship. I don't want to date." Her bare foot was working my dick, and I swear this woman could do things with her toes that nearly made me bust the zipper on my good slacks. "I don't even want tomorrow," she continued. "All I want is you, *preferably naked.*"

I stilled her extremely skilled foot with one hand and raised the other to call for the check. Later, I'd have to remember to thank Ned for *finally* breaking me off some good advice. This was exactly what I needed, and judging by what Kiara could do to a dick with just her foot, I was well on my way to forgetting all about Alex Bridges.

Kiara had met me at the restaurant, so she drove her own ride to my house. My place hadn't been my first choice, but she was staying with her parents until she closed on a new condo. Besides, it was obvious Kiara and I wanted the same thing out of tonight, and she didn't appear to be the type to linger after we got it.

I parked in my driveway, and my gaze automatically traveled next door. Alex's car was there. I didn't see her, but the lights were on inside her place illuminating the darkness. I looked away. Despite all my grown man talk, I felt a twinge of something that felt a hell of a lot like guilt.

So don't do it. Kiara hasn't even gotten out of her car yet. You can still send her home.

Nah. An attack of conscience over a woman I'm not even with is exactly why I *should* do this.

Then another thought occurred to me. Alex might be out of sight, but that didn't mean there wasn't a surprise awaiting me in our ongoing feud. I got out of my car and glanced around my yard and house.

Nothing. At least, nothing I could see, *yet.*

"You okay?"

I'd been so busy scouting for possible booby traps left by my neighbor that I hadn't heard Kiara walk up behind me. I did another scan of my surroundings before smiling down at her. "Yeah, I'm good."

Kiara inclined her head toward my house and raised a brow. "You sure there isn't a wife or girlfriend that you thought would be out on the other side of that door?"

I assured her I had neither, but didn't feel entirely comfortable until we were inside. It was only in the safety of my living room that I allowed myself a long and very appreciative look at Kiara and her banging yoga body.

"Like what you see?" She slid her tongue over her bottom lip again.

"Mmm, mmm." I reached for her, but she took a step back.

Crossing her arms, she grasped the hem of her cropped top and pulled it up and over her head putting the breasts I'd been staring at all through dinner on full view. And from the looks of those brown pebbled nipples she was either cold or excited to be here.

Seeing as how I didn't have air conditioning and the breeze floating through the house's open windows was mild, I didn't think she was cold. Not at all.

"Ready to take this to your bedroom?"

I nodded, having heard her, but my eyeballs weren't on her face right now.

Kiara tossed the top aside and laughed. "Then lead the way."

Seeing as how you're solidly #TeamAlex, I won't trouble you with the preliminaries, not that they were that many. Our clothes were scattered across the floor, and my hands were all over that sexy yoga body. Kiara's response to just my touch was enthusiastic *and boisterous*. Within minutes, I was rolling on a condom as she got on her hands and knees in the center of my bed. Face down, ass up.

Oh, yeah.

Dick in hand, I joined her on the bed ready to hit that ass from the back.

Instead, it hit me – with a big, fat, loud fart.

Ewwwwww!

My dick shrank inside the condom as an odor that rivaled all the sulfur in hell quickly filled the room. I jumped off the bed, but not before my eyebrows melted and slid off my face.

Good Lawd! What had this woman been eating?

That bean bowl popped into my head as I gagged and tears formed in my eyes. I headed for the window to suck in a breath.

Oh, shit!

Gulping in air, I noticed the close proximity of my bedroom window to next door. My neighbor claimed to have heard me snoring, but she'd just been messing around. Nah, Alex couldn't have heard.

Another rancid fart erupted from Kiera's pert behind, even louder (think string of exploding Chinese firecrackers) and smellier than the first. I heard a burst of laughter coming from Alex's window followed by more of her damned laughing. My burning nostrils were messing with my mind, I reasoned. Alex was probably just tuned in to tonight's *Black-ish* marathon. Yeah, that was it.

You don't really believe that, do you?

Shut up.

Needless to say, the sex with Kiara wasn't happening. She'd left in a huff after accusing me of not being able to handle an all-natural woman. I immediately stripped the sheets and comforter from my bed. Bypassing the laundry room, I tossed them outside onto the back porch. I'd buy new linen tomorrow, and it was very possible, I'd have to repaint my bedroom walls.

In the meantime, I'd sleep on the couch.

What happened to the big, bad, grown assed man?

That toxic funk cloud broke him down to the fetal position.

It serves you right for trying to cheat on Alex.

I was not cheating on Alex! How many times do I have to tell you that I'm an unattached, grown assed... Oh, just forget it. I'm going to sleep.

14

"I didn't choose the obnoxious-neighbor life.
The obnoxious-neighbor life chose me."

ALEX

THUNDER SHOOK the hardwood floors beneath my feet as I stared out of my living room window watching a now familiar SUV slow down long enough for an arm to haphazardly fling the newspaper into my neighbor's front yard.

By now I would have already dashed outside like an eager puppy to retrieve it, but wind-whipped rain pounded my front porch, and except for streaks of lightening, the dark skies looked more dusk than dawn. I heard a long beep from the television in the other room, and the news anchor announced another severe weather alert for an adjacent county.

Damn.

I'd been looking forward to my daily encounter with my neighbor, this morning especially.

Girl, you look forward to seeing Justice Lawson every morning.

Unfortunately, you're right, and my fiasco of a date last night did little to change things. But that's not what you really want to know, is it? Nope. You're dying to know what I did or didn't hear coming from my neighbor's bedroom window last night.

Well, first of all, due to...

Don't roll your eyes and tell me to just spit it out. This is my story, and I'll tell it in my own good time. Now I'll have to start again at the beginning.

So as I was saying, due to the close proximity of our houses, I'd grown used to hearing Lawson's car engine as he came and went. It was the female voice that got my attention. I'd told myself the woman was just a friend, but their body language said different, and the sight of them standing in his yard hit me with an emotion I hadn't expected. I also had no right to feel any kind of way, considering I'd just come from a date that I had fully intended to turn into a one-night stand.

Yeah, I'd been jealous.

At the time, I wished that I'd taken time to make another move in my feud with Lawson. Something that would have sent that cute chick with the pixie cut speeding away from Old Trail Avenue and away from...

Your man?

Scratch that thought. Justice Lawson's love life is no business of mine, and you know full well he is not my man. And FYI, I don't need you butting in trying to finish my sentences.

Then for goodness sake get to the point. Did you or did you not overhear what went down in Justice's bedroom last night?

CRASH!

Hold that thought. I have to go outside and investigate that godawful racket.

I grabbed an umbrella on my way out the door. However, the wind quickly rendered it useless, first turning it inside out and then snatching it completely from my grasp. Shit! Shit Shit! Rain pelting me, I trudged around to the side of my house, mud invading into my sneakers with every step. I stopped short and stared open-mouthed at the source of the noise.

The ladder that had been leaning against my house was now jammed right through my neighbor's bedroom window.

Justice!

Panic knotting my insides, I took off in the direction of my neighbor's front door only to slam into a wall of a chest. I looked up from the soaking wet t-shirt covering well-defined pectorals to the hard planes of Justice's face. Thank goodness. He was okay. I resisted the urge to run my hands down his arms and over his broad chest to make sure he wasn't hurt.

My relief didn't last long.

"What the hell?" Lawson bellowed.

I followed my neighbor's glare back to the ladder protruding through his broken window.

"The storm," I yelled over the rain in way of explanation, but was drowned out by thunder.

Water ran in rivulets down Lawson's angry face. "You did this. It's all *your* fault!"

"My fault?" Was this man out of his mind? Did he not notice it was storming? "As badly as I want to get rid of you, I can't take credit for ramming a ladder through your window. So chalk this one up to Mother Nature."

"If you had put your damn ladder away, it wouldn't be hanging out of my window right now," he said. "And that is your property, correct?" Lawson inclined his head toward the same scrawl I'd read to him a few days ago. "Property of Tate Bridges," he mimicked my voice.

The rain continued to beat down on us as our war of words escalated.

"You're paying for this Bridges. New window, water damage, the entire mess, I'll be handing you a bill for all of it."

"You might as well send that bill to your insurance company, because this was an accident. I'm not paying for a damn thing."

Lawson snorted. "Just like a Bridges."

Oblivious to the storm, I toed up to him, until there were just inches of space between us. "What in the hell is that supposed to mean?"

"You know what it means," he said. "This feud wouldn't have even started all those years ago if you

Bridges would have taken responsibility and paid for your screw up."

I stared at him incredulous. "Seriously? You're dumping the reason for this stupid feud at *my* family's doorstep. You ever think that if your great, great, great grandparents' mule hadn't been so hot to trot there wouldn't have even been a feud. Your family should have kept a better eye on your livestock."

"How were my ancestors to know that your Bridges's mule would break down the fence separating our yards and fuck the Lawson's mule to death?" Justice asked, as our argument regressed to the early twentieth century. "Then just like you're doing right now, use Mother Nature as an excuse not to pay damages. Not this time, Bridges. You're paying for my window!"

"And if I don't?" Crossing my arms over my chest, I raised a brow. "What are you going to do, fart until your stench sends me running for my life like it did your poor date last night?"

I watched with satisfaction as my neighbor's jaw dropped and his face turned an interesting shade of purple. "T-that wasn't me," he stammered. "It was..."

"Mmm, hmm," I interrupted. "That's what they all say, *Stinky*."

To be honest, I knew Lawson hadn't been the one with the *digestion issues*, but *he* didn't know that.

My neighbor started in on me again, apparently recovered from his momentary embarrassment. "You seem to be paying extraordinary attention to what's going down at my house. Perhaps that ladder is there because you were peeping through my bedroom window."

"Don't be ridiculous."

"Maybe you're simply jealous because I had a date," he said. "Or is it that you want me so bad you can't stand it?"

That particular accusation hit a sore spot too close to the truth, but I wasn't about to let him see it. "You wish, Lawson. I'd take a walk through hell with gasoline drawers before I'd go on a date with you."

"Do you hear me asking you on one?"

Shaking with fury, I opened my mouth to tell him I wasn't going to stand outside in this weather having this conversation, when I realized the rain had stopped and the dark sky had suddenly brightened. "I'm going inside. I'll come back and get that stupid—"

"Quiet!" Lawson barked, as he stared up at the sky. "We need to get out—"

"Who do you think you're telling to be quiet?" This man must be off his meds talking to me like that.

Thunder rumbled like an oncoming train in the distance, despite the clear skies.

"You'd better—" Before I could finish the thought, Lawson scooped me up and tossed me over his shoulder caveman style. The quick move knocked my next breath from my lungs with a whoosh. "What in the hell do you think you're doing? Have you lost your mind?" I pummeled his broad back with my fists. "Put me down, right this minute, Lawson! Put me down!"

My neighbor was too busy running toward his backyard still carrying me like a sack of potatoes to heed my protests. The wind had picked up again and debris had started falling from the now eerily green skies. I raised my torso off Lawson's back just as a siren sounded, and then I saw what he'd known was coming moments before. A huge funnel cloud was swirling up Old Trail Avenue headed right at us.

"Tornado," I screamed, just as Lawson put me on my feet.

"Wrap your arms around me and hang on tight," he yelled.

I did as he instructed. The wind roared around us like an enraged wild animal. It stung my eyes and it felt like it would rip the clothes off my back. Justice threw open what looked like a trap door and without preliminary, grabbed me by the arm and threw me into a pit. My ass hit the hard concrete at the bottom of it. Stunned, I watched Lawson wrestle the elements to slam the door closed and secure it.

He'd saved me.

The thought echoed in my mind as the door vibrated above us as if it were about to be snatched from its hinges. My neighbor switched on a lantern, and I blinked against the harsh LED light. Glancing around the small space, which consisted of shelves on one side and a cot on the other, I surmised we were in the underground storm cellar I vaguely remembered Lawson mentioning to my mother the day I'd moved in.

"You okay?" He pulled me to my feet and immediately ran his hands down my arms to check for himself.

Just like I'd longed to do to him earlier. "I'm sorry I shoved you so hard, but that funnel was headed right for..."

As if on cue, the cellar door rattled violently, and it sounded like all hell was breaking loose above us. Looking up, I gnawed at my bottom lip.

"Don't worry." Lawson's hands were still on my arms as he followed my gaze. "This cellar and our houses have survived over a hundred years of storms and twisters."

I hadn't gotten that far. Despite the fact that we'd been hurling insults and accusations at each other with a viciousness that would have made our feuding ancestors proud, I was still stuck on how this man had gotten us *both* to safety.

"You saved me," I said aloud. My voice quivered with the realization. "All you had to do was save yourself. There's no way I could have survived what's going on above us right now. I would have been gone for good. Feud over." Call me slow, but I was still stunned and confused. "What was it, your conscience or something?"

"No." Lawson shook his head, his handsome face unreadable. "It wasn't my conscience."

"I don't understand. You could have finally had everything you ever wanted."

"Not everything." Holding my gaze with an intensity rivaling the winds swirling above, Lawson took my face between his palms. I sighed into his mouth as he proceeded to kiss the hell out of me.

YAAAAAS! Finally!

Tell me about it.

So is it everything you thought it would be?

Lawd, yes!

Hmm, mmm. That fine assed Justice seemed the type to melt panties with a single kiss. And he is about to get the panties, right?

Do you mind? All the questions are killing the vibe.

All too soon the kiss was over. My knees were straight jelly, but I somehow managed not to sag against Lawson's big body for support. His dark eyes possessed the same intensity as he stared down at me, and I swallowed a lump of emotion caught in my throat.

"But what about the..." I began.

The man I'd been locked in an ongoing battle with rested a gentle finger against my lips, which still trembled from his kiss. "The tornado siren sounded too late. If we hadn't been outside, if I hadn't spotted that funnel, it would have been too late for both of us, *period*." He glanced down as if he were trying to compose himself. When he looked at me again, the planes of his face were hard, his eyes serious. "Fuck that feud!"

I blinked, startled by both his declaration and its raw ferocity.

He kissed me again. My fingers fisted the t-shirt stretched across his broad chest. His mouth commanded mine, and I sank deeper into him, feeling every stroke of his tongue down to my toes, which curled inside my wet sneakers. My sneakers weren't the only thing wet, considering the sizeable dick pressed against my belly.

I was breathless when we came up for air. My fists clung to his shirt, and I itched to do what the wind had tried and failed, rip the clothes off his back. Though you wouldn't know it from the way I was behaving, Alexandra Bridges wasn't the type of woman to melt at a man's feet after a kiss or two. Even if I had been lusting over him for weeks.

Catching my breath, I struggled to regain the cool he'd shaken. "So you're conceding, Lawson?" I raised a brow.

A smirk twisted his dark features as he grasped my arms. His thumbs brushed over my breasts in the process leaving their peaks so hard they ached. I bit my bottom lip to stem the wave of longing elicited by his touch.

"Yeah, total surrender." Lawson's gaze fell to my chest, and his mouth followed, tugging a nipple between his teeth and then laving it with his tongue. "So what's it going to be, Bridges, *sworn enemies or lovers?*"

I already had my answer, but after feuding for weeks I couldn't make it so damn easy for him. Flattening my palms against his chest, I pushed lightly against it. "The last time something belonging to a Bridges sexed Lawson property, it couldn't handle it and died."

My rescuer threw his head back and laughed, a full, rich sound that vibrated through me managing to simultaneously soak my panties and make my heart skip a beat.

"Don't laugh, Lawson. It's been a long time for me, it could happen."

"I'll take my chances."

My gaze dropped to his erection. I bit my bottom lip to keep from licking it.

Licking what?

Never you mind.

I tried unsuccessfully to peel my eyeballs from his crotch. "You're packing, Lawson. I'll give you that, but can you work that *generous* equipment skillfully enough to make me forget our feud, not to mention forfeit three-hundred grand?"

Lawson raised a brow as if to ask *is that all?*' Then he nodded once, his expression confident. "I gotchu."

Dayum! I suppressed an urge to fan myself, but couldn't stop the big grin splitting my face in half. "Then drop those jeans and bring me that three hundred thousand dollar dick."

15

"When you're feuding with a Bridges, it's not over until it's over"

JUSTICE

THE FIRST RULE to surrendering your position in a hundred-year old feud is to honor the other side's demand.

That's how Alex wound up naked and pinned to the cellar's cot with those long, gorgeous legs draped over my shoulders.

"Please." She squirmed beneath me. Her breathless plea went straight to my dick, and it was all I could do not to plunge inside her balls deep. I held back. Blocking out the almost painful disapproval of my raging hard on.

Geezus, what are you waiting on? Hit it!

Look, both you and my dick are going to have to slow your roll. This isn't like the last time you saw me with a woman. I've wanted Alex Bridges from the moment we met, and I'm not doing a rush job. The setting wasn't ideal, but I'd waited for this too long, wanted it too badly not to savor it.

Now if you don't mind, I have freckles to address.

Alex squirmed again. "I'm covered in freckles. Exactly how many do you plan to kiss?"

I raised my head from her flat belly, where I'd just kissed one freckle, and then licked another. "Every damn one of them." I kissed a freckle on her hipbone and licked the one occupying the space beside it on her satin soft skin. The woman tasted just as good as she looked, and even on a day like today, she made me think of lemonade and sunshine.

Alex rose to her elbows. Ignoring the pretty pout on her face, I inched lower and pressed my lips to a spot on her inner thigh.

"If freckle business is all you're interested in handling, I'm not feeling putting an end to this feud," she huffed.

I looked up from the freckle I'd just licked and raised a brow. "You sure about that, Bridges?"

"Absolutely."

"We'll see." Time to handle pussy business. Lowering my head, I moved in and slid my tongue over her clit in a long, languid lick.

"Yasssss!" Alex hissed.

Her hips bucked, and I cupped her ass in my hands to steady her before she threw us both to the concrete floor. I swirled my tongue over the same spot and let it linger as her soft pants filled the enclosed space.

Pausing, I raised my head, the rest of my body struggling to maintain control. "Is this feud over?"

"Mmm..."

I licked her again, long and slow, and then pulled back as she squirmed for more. "I didn't quite catch that."

"Mmm, hmm."

Stubborn assed, Bridges. I was putting an end to this feud, right here, right now, if my dick didn't explode first. Sucking her clit into my mouth I worked it with my tongue until her thighs started to tremble. Then I pulled back.

"I asked you a question." I kissed the inside of her thigh. "And I expect an answer."

Alex's muttered curse burned my ears, and she tried it with squeezing her thighs together to hold my head in place. Extricating my head from their grip, I licked her again.

"Is." Lick. "This." Swirl. "Feud" Lick. "Done?"

"*God, yes!*" Alex screamed her reply as she came on my tongue. "It's done! It's done!"

Moments later, I hovered over her, a condom from the wallet in my discarded jeans on my rock hard dick. "Now I believe I'm still three-hundred thousand dollars in your debt."

Alex smiled as her glance traveled from my dick to my face. "Then it's time you pay what you owe."

16

"You can't always judge a Bridges by their family."

JUSTICE

THE SOUND of engines and voices from above ground grew louder and closer to the cellar door I hadn't been able to push open earlier. I shrugged my shoulder to nudge the woman sound asleep on my chest awake.

"They're finally coming for us." I stroked knuckles down her cheek, and then raised my back off the concrete wall. "Wake up, Alex."

Her eyelids fluttered open, and I caught a glimpse of the eyes that would forever make me think of only one Tate Bridges. A smile lit up her face, and part of me wished I could hold off the swiftly approaching outside world a while longer.

While I'd meant everything I'd said and done while we'd rode out the storm – and each other, I didn't know for sure if it had been the same for Alex. "Look, I understand about being in the heat of the moment. So if you feel differently about both the feud and the money once ..."

Alex shushed me with a finger across my lips. "If there's one thing this feud has proved, it's that we're both smart, capable, and badass enough to make our own money," she said finally. "You're a formidable enemy, Justice Lawson, but I believe we're better together as allies."

Pulling her to me, I kissed her in a way that left no doubt how I felt about that idea.

"Justice! You down there?" I heard Ned's panicked voice, and it sounded like whatever was blocking the door was being removed.

I yelled back to let him know I was indeed in the storm cellar.

"Hang on," Ned called out. "We're coming for you."

Minutes later, the cellar door creaked open. Daylight poured into the small space, and a guy wearing a Nashville Fire Department helmet looked down at us. "You two need us to come get you out."

Assuring him we were both fine, I helped Alex up first, and then climbed out of the cellar. Red and blue lights from emergency vehicles flashed all around us, but they dimmed in the light of Ned's relieved face.

"Man, am I glad to see y'all." He slapped me on the back. "I was scared shitless when I couldn't get you on the phone after the storm, and then got out here, and both you and Alex were nowhere in sight..."

Ned's voice faded into the background and I looked around. My face mirrored the stricken expression I saw on Alex's.

"The houses," she gasped.

I looked from the spot where the house, my family had poured their lifeblood into had once stood to the space Alex's ancestral home had occupied just this morning. Now they were both gone.

Just like that.

After all these years, they'd finally encountered a storm neither could withstand. Now only their ancient foundations remained. The rest had been reduced to rubble that was strewn across the other side of the street.

"Well, I'll be damned," I muttered, then turned to Alex. "Do you know what this..."

Ned cut me off. "You sure you two don't need the medics to check you out?" Concerned laced his tone.

"I'm good." Alex pushed out a sigh. "Homeless, but otherwise okay."

"We managed to get to safety just in time," I explained.

Ned raised a brow, and then shook his head. "That tornado must have really done a number on y'all before you made it down into the cellar." He pointed at us. "Just look at you. Your shirt is ripped as if the storm tried to tear it off your back. Alex's is on backwards, and her hair looks like..." He stopped abruptly as realization dawned in his eyes. A grin on his face, he pointed again, this time from me to Alex and back at me again. "Does this mean y'all are together?"

Alex and I reached for each other's hands simultaneously. I wrapped my larger hand around hers, and then seemingly out of nowhere that old garden gnome rolled toward us. It stopped at Alex's feet, and if I didn't know any better, I'd say its wizened face was glaring in disapproval.

"So after all these years, the Bridges – Lawson feud is really over?" Ned asked.

I started to answer, when Alex reached down and picked up that old, ugly gnome. She stared at it a long moment, and then threw it with all her might. It landed on the piles of rubble across the street and shattered into pieces.

"Yeah, the feud is over." Alex smiled up at me, and then looked at the empty space where our houses once stood. "We may not have anything else, but we have each other."

I raised her hand to my lips and kissed it. "Not exactly."

"Huh?" Alex scrunched up her nose in confusion.

"We aren't broke, Bridges," I informed her. "In fact, if I'm right, we both have checks to collect."

17

---

*"I like my Lawson the same as my coffee – strong, black
and able to keep me awake all night long."*

ALEX

AFTER WE GOT out of the cellar, Justice did two things
that made me very happy.

Justice, huh?

Yeah, it's like that between us these days.

Well, spit it out. What did he do?

First, he reminded me that because we no longer had
houses we could both claim our feud clause inheritances
immediately. How awesome is that?

*Both of you are big money now, huh? So that means
y'all are going to be doing big things.*

Not yet. We're taking it slow. In fact, Justice asked me out on our first date. He's taking me on a picnic – in Central Park.

"Delta Airlines is now boarding this morning's non-stop flight from Nashville to New York City. Passengers holding first-class tickets are welcome to board."

Justice stood and held out his hand. "You ready, babe?"

I nodded and placed my hand in his.

So what's next for you two?

Like I said, we're taking it slow. I promised not to leave him stranded on a hot roof. He promised not to get grass in my 'fro. You know, relationship goals.

ACKNOWLEDGMENTS

Love and gratitude to Michelle, Marika, Christina and Patience for their wisdom, encouragement and friendship.

And as always, thanks to Mr. Phyllis – the best editor ever!

BETWEEN A ROCK & A HOT MESS

Excerpt from BOOK ONE of the Sinclair Brides series
NOW AVAILABLE

1

RILEY

An unladylike snort escaped from between my lips, earning a frown from my sister.

"Oh, Riley." Hope shook her head, sighed, and tsked me.

The way my family tossed it around, you would think the word *Oh* accompanied by a disapproving huff was my name. Actually, it's Riley Sinclair, and I did not gloat.

Okay, maybe I had just a bit, but under the circumstances, who could blame me? The man was annoying as hell and had deserved everything I could dish out, and more. "It's called w-i-n-n-i-n-g." I spelled the word out slowly in an attempt to school my sister on how to handle a victory, but it was a wasted effort.

Still, nothing could steal the triumphant thrill of Sinclair Construction's softball team handing Mills

Plumbing their ass this evening in a seven-to-two beat-down. I glanced around the dining room of First Down sports bar, where my crew was enjoying celebratory bottles of beer as they awaited pizza and wings on the company tab. Then I met my sister's sanctimonious side-eye.

"We weren't even playing Parker Construction. Hudson Parker was only there to watch the game."

Hope threw up her hands. She didn't play on the company team, thank God. However, she still came out to cheer us on. "You had no call whatsoever to go bull-dozing into the stands to rub his nose in the win. It was unprofessional and unsportsmanlike, not to mention a totally ungracious move on your part."

Ungracious. I rolled my eyes so hard they nearly bounced off the ceiling. "I'm reserving my nonexistent manners for tea with the queen. As far as being unprofes-sional goes, we're off the clock. So there's nothing wrong with letting the head of Parker Construction know he can expect the same kind of whipping if our teams face off in the championship game."

My sister sticking up for the enemy was even more irksome than her criticism of my so-called unsportsman-like behavior. "Besides, I'm the boss. Who's going to check me?"

"You're so rude." Hope shuddered and took a sip from her lemon-adorned glass of mineral water. "If Mom had witnessed your bad behavior, she would have checked you, all right." She leveled a glossy French-mani-cured fingertip in my direction. "You may run the work crews, Riley Sinclair, but she owns the company and is therefore the boss of you."

Well, she had me there. All I could do was grunt and take a swig of my beer. Hope and our mother sat behind desks in the air-conditioned offices of our company's headquarters. What did they know? Neither of them were outdoors on the front line checking on our various job sites around town. Not once had they ever had to swing a hammer or take the wheel of a backhoe.

"Besides, it's only a stupid game," she continued. "The point of the company participating in recreational league sports is to foster camaraderie and have fun."

"Just a game?"

I stared at my sister slack-jawed before looking down at my jersey, dirt-stained from my dive for home plate. I zeroed in on the red, green, and white emblem of the company started by our late father. Like a talisman, it reinforced the lessons on competitiveness and killer instinct he'd ingrained in me as the oldest of his daughters.

I was about to remind my prim-and-proper sibling how important our company's softball and bowling teams and *winning* had been to him when the waitress placed a large pizza in the center of the table.

Hope topped our plates with the first slices before I could grab mine. I used my hands to lift a topping-laden slice from my half to my mouth. My sister unwrapped cutlery from a napkin, and then began to cut her slice from the cheese-only side of the pizza into perfect bite-size portions. No matter how many times I'd watched her do it, the sight of Hope eating pizza, buffalo wings, and even hamburgers with a knife and fork always threw me.

Silence reigned at the table as we spent the next few moments focusing on our food. Despite our differences, the one thing the Sinclair sisters had in common were healthy appetites and a deep appreciation of mealtime.

After downing two slices, I reached for another and got back to the topic at hand. "This was way more than just a game. It's a point of pride, and so was rubbing Hudson Parker's nose in it."

Hope shrugged. "The guy seems okay to me, and not too bad on the eyes. If you weren't so busy complaining about him, you might notice that the man is fine."

"Ha!" I practically barked. "Yeah, he's fine, all right. Fine with trying to steal business from us. Fine with taking the food right out of our mouths."

Hope eyed me over the rim of her water glass as she took a sip. "Nashville is booming. There's enough new construction going on here to provide business and food for all of us. Besides, business isn't what's got you so worked up, and you know it. You're still mad Parker Construction won last year's first-place softball trophy, as well as last fall's bowling league championship."

"Both those bowling and softball trophies had been in Sinclair Construction's hands for yours, before his company showed up in town and pulled together teams," I argued.

"*Winning* teams," Hope amended.

A fact that continued to rankle me. "He'd better savor those past victories, because they're the only ones he's going to get. And there's absolutely nothing wrong with warning him that our team is coming for that ass."

"Riley!" Hope admonished.

"It's the truth."

"Lighten up, Riley. You too, Miss Priss." The metallic jangle of bracelets accompanied a familiar voice, as our friend, Plum, plopped down in the empty chair at our table and adjusted her gauzy, tie-dye skirt.

Sugar Plum Watson (her government name) had grown up next door to us and knew the Sinclair sisters nearly as well as we knew each other. She also refused to hold a conversation with anyone who called her by her first name.

Plum shrugged her tote bag off her shoulder onto the floor and helped herself to pizza, not bothering with a plate. She signaled the waitress and ordered a diet cola and a salad before turning her attention to me. "How'd the game go?"

"We won."

"Good," she nodded. "We won't have to listen to your sore loser bellyaching all evening."

"But I'm not a sore..."

The matching looks on Plum and Hope's faces stopped me midsentence. I can argue with the best of them, but not when I'm dead wrong. I relayed the game highlights to Plum, who appeared more interested in the salad the waitress had slid in front of her than my softball game.

"This win puts us one step closer to getting that trophy back," I said.

"You mean closer to shoving it in Hudson Parker's face," Hope clarified.

Plum looked up from her salad, fork poised midair. "Who's he?"

"A guy on another team Riley was rude to earlier."

Plum smirked. "Riley, rude. What else is new?"

"I know, right?" my sister asked rhetorically, and they shared a laugh at my expense.

"Oh, I have something to show you." Plum abandoned her food, reached into her tote bag and retrieved a magazine. The thick glossy landed on the table with a thud.

I caught sight of the cover. A woman with a death grip on a pink bouquet stared up from it. She was swathed in white satin and her teeth shone like high beams on a dark road.

Plum flipped through the pages of the bridal magazine, stopping on one she'd flagged with a Post-it note. She shoved it in my sister's direction. "I think these bridesmaid dresses are exactly what you've been looking for."

Hope's eyes went soft as she looked at the magazine, and her face took on the expression she wore whenever anything to do with her upcoming nuptials came up. "Oh, my God, they're gorgeous."

I averted my gaze from the page of pale-pink dresses, hoping the twinge of envy I felt deep down wasn't visible. With the recent engagements of Hope and Plum, it seemed as if everyone I knew was now engaged, married, or cohabiting with a significant other in a state of domestic bliss.

Plum commandeered the magazine and flipped to another flagged page. "And I think something like this might work for my wedding gown." She pointed to a model wearing a dress so frothy it looked like whipped cream, and then to the red dresses beside it. "Maybe these for my bridesmaids, seeing as how we're having a Christmas holiday wedding."

"What?" Hope's mouth dropped open. "I thought you had your heart set on autumn."

Plum launched into a lengthy explanation. It wasn't exactly a surprise to learn her future mother-in-law had demanded the change and her son had followed suit. "Doug wants to make his mom happy, and when you're part of a couple, you have to compromise." Tension marred her forced smile as she pointed to a green lace dress. "Or maybe this one for the bridesmaids?"

I unleashed a yawn that pretty much summed up my feelings on the subject. "Come on, you two aren't going to ruin my softball victory with a bunch of talk about dresses and wedding whatnot, are you?"

The smile Hope wore while ogling the pages of the magazine turned into a frown when she looked up at me. "You might want to pay attention to this *whatnot*, since you're the maid of honor in both of our weddings and will be wearing these dresses."

"Humph." I sat back in my chair and took another swig of beer.

"Oh, Riley," Hope chastised. She shook her head as she reached for her mineral water.

Plum, on the other hand, wasn't fooled by my show of bravado. I averted my eyes hoping to shield my thoughts, but it was too late.

My friend stretched an arm across the table and covered my free hand with hers. "Your turn will come, Riley," she said softly.

"Oh, no. I'm not looking to have my life revolve around some man's whims. Y'all can have that." I tried to pull my hand away to brush off her observation, but she tightened her grip.

Plum's perceptive gaze, the same one that had peered at me through countless birthday and slumber parties, knew better. She knew how it hurt me to always be the girl that boys thought of as a friend, but never a girl-friend. She knew that although I was happy for her and my sister, it would be tough for me to watch them both get married next year, when I didn't even have a prospect.

"There's a guy out there for you," she continued. "One who will appreciate how independent and capable you are, and absolutely adore you."

"She'd probably scare him off with her total lack of tact," Hope interjected.

She had a point. Men who weren't turned off by the fact I didn't look like the women who were currently in vogue—petite, waif thin, spackled in makeup with plastic boobs and a weave hanging down to my backside—didn't like my outspokenness. Nor had I met one that made me want to refrain from breaking off some real talk where I thought it was needed.

Plum shook her head. "I disagree," she said. "Riley's true Prince Charming will love everything about her, including her occasional obnoxiousness."

My longtime friend's words managed to slip through the tough hide of my defenses. I cleared my throat. "Do you really think so?"

What I had said before was true. I would never be the kind of woman whose life revolved around providing her man with a lifetime of maid and nanny service. Nor did I envy Plum's choice of a mama's boy, or the cheap bastard Hope had selected to be my future brother-in-law.

I didn't even want a big, splashy wedding. Still, I couldn't help but wonder if I'd ever have my own happily-ever-after...

Plum patted my hand before finally releasing it. "Of course you will," she said, as if she'd read my mind. "It's only a matter of time before you encounter a man who recognizes how utterly fabulous you are and we're all eating red velvet cake pops at your wedding reception."

The mention of my favorite dessert paled in comparison to the sparkle of the diamond solitaire on her left hand.

"If she doesn't bite his head off first." Something caught Hope's attention, and she looked beyond me toward the sports bar's front door. "Speak of the devil. It looks like one of your favorite victims just walked in."

"Who?" Plum and I asked simultaneously, both turning in our chairs toward the door.

Hudson Parker. What was he doing here?

"Damn," Plum said in a hushed tone. "If I wasn't engaged, I wouldn't mind taking a bite out of him."

"He's quite handsome in a rugged kind of way," Hope chimed in.

I swiveled in my seat, refusing to look at him a second longer than necessary. "What he is, is a giant pain in my ass."

"Well, don't look now, big sister, but that ache in your posterior is headed this way."

"Every fine inch of him," Plum murmured. "What is he, six-three, six-four?"

"Definitely, six-four," Hope said.

"Shouldn't you be focused on your fiancé's height?" I snapped at my sister.

A long shadow loomed over the table. I scowled at its owner, while the two engaged women surrounding me stared up at him in awestruck, Idris Elba–worthy wonder. They were going gaga at the sight of Hudson Parker, of all people. Unbelievable. I resisted the urge to stick my finger down my throat.

"Evening, ladies."

Plum sighed at the sound of his deep baritone. A simpering little smile graced my prissy sister's lips.

"Riley." He inclined his head in my direction. The gesture made it clear the first greeting was reserved for the other two women at the table.

"What do you want, Parker?"

"Riley!" Hope scolded, but she was wasting her breath.

Arching a brow, I crossed my arms over my chest and waited for his answer. He may have lulled by sister and best friend into a trance with those broad shoulders and muscles straining against the confines of his black T-shirt. Or maybe it was the chiseled face, square jaw, and skin baked to a deep shade of bronze by the sun.

It didn't affect me. I worked with his type all day long, so I wasn't as easily taken in or impressed. "Well?" I prodded.

"Can't a guy just come over and say hello?" he asked. "It's not as if we're strangers."

"We're not friends, either. I've already said all I have to say to you today, so why don't you...Ow!" A sharp pain in my leg that felt like a kick stopped me midsentence. I knew the sensible heel of Hope's pump was the culprit. "What did you kick me for?" I rubbed the sore spot where her shoe had connected with my shin.

She ignored the question. Meanwhile, Plum introduced herself and motioned toward the empty chair between us. "Would you like to join us, Mr. Parker?"

He ran his tongue over his full bottom lip before biting down on it with even white teeth, as if he were actually contemplating it. I guess the fact that if he had his way, Sinclair Construction would be out of business was lost on my best friend and sister.

Hope flashed him one of her polite, proper smiles. "There's plenty of pizza," she coaxed.

I leveled the man with a stare, so he'd know exactly what I thought of the idea. He may have had everyone else at the table mesmerized, but not me. "Too bad I can't fart right now."

"Riley!" My sister gasped.

Plum's face contorted into a frown. "Aw, Riley. We're trying to eat here."

In contrast, an amused smile touched Parker's lips and traveled up to his dark-brown eyes. I suppressed a pulse of awareness between my thighs that made me forget about the pain still radiating from my shin.

What the hell?

Hope and Plum's silliness must be contagious, I reasoned. No way anything about this man could turn me on.

"Perhaps, another time, ladies." He was talking to them, but his gaze remained on me. I held it without blinking, hoping to convey the message that I wasn't intimidated by him. *Or attracted.* "See you around, Riley."

"The next thing you'll see is the sight of one of my home-run balls sailing over your head," I said. "That is, if Parker Construction even makes the playoffs."

His smile deepened at the taunt, revealing a dimple in his left cheek. "Oh, we'll make the playoffs, all right. In fact, I'm confident the league's first-place trophy will remain in my office for another year," he said. "Be nice, and I may let you visit it."

"Riley be nice? Fat chance of that happening," Hope said as he walked away.

Both her and Plum's eyeballs were glued to his jean-clad behind as he sauntered across the room to join some of my crew, as well as players from Mills Plumbing, who were all watching a baseball game at the bar.

I snapped my fingers to rouse them from their trance and pointed to the wedding magazine they'd been poring over before the interruption. "Too bad your husbands-to-be aren't around to see you two bridezillas ogling ass."

"I-I was doing no such thing," Hope stammered in a weak protest. "Just because I don't act like I was raised in a barn, like you."

"Moo," I deadpanned.

Plum pointed a finger in Parker's direction. I followed it, relieved to see his back was to us. The last thing I wanted was for the man to think he was the topic of any conversation I participated in.

"Now *that*, Riley, is Prince Charming material," she said.

Unfortunately, I'd picked that moment to take a sip from my beer. "W-what?" I sputtered incredulously. "You must have lost your damn mind."

Hope nodded. "I'm inclined to agree with my sister for a change. She can't stand him."

"Are you blind?" Plum directed her question at me. "That man is hot. What do you have against tall, dark, and delicious anyway?"

I grunted. "More like slick, annoying, and ruthless. Besides, he's the competition. The man stole two big jobs from us."

"Sinclair Construction never had those jobs," Hope corrected. "His company won those bids fair and square."

"We would have if he hadn't thrown his hard hat into the mix."

Plum shrugged. "So you two are in the same business. It gives you something in common."

I glanced at the now-cold pizza with its congealing cheese. Another slice of it would be preferable to the turn this conversation had taken.

"He's not my type." That much was true. He was as far away from being the type of man I wanted as Nashville was from Paris (the city in France, not the small Tennessee town a little over a hundred miles away).

"Shame." Plum stared across the room at Parker and then shrugged, apparently satisfied with my answer.

Hope, on the other hand, was not. "I don't get you at all. One minute you're looking like the only kid on the block with no ice cream, because everyone is paired off except you. The next, you're saying a man, who if you ask me is crazy about your rude behind, isn't your type."

Crazy about me? Huh? It was no secret that Hope was a lightweight when it came to alcohol. Clearly she had something else in her drink besides water.

"Nobody asked you. Besides, that's the stupidest thing I've heard all day."

Hope lifted a brow. "Maybe, but I saw the way he looked at you before you ran him off."

My sister was off her rocker. Parker viewed me the same way I saw him, as unfriendly competition. That's all. "I already told you, he isn't my type."

She pursed her lips. "Then how about telling us exactly what your type *is*?"

Plum leaned forward in her chair, awaiting my answer. They'd obviously thought the question would stump me, but I not only knew the type of man I wanted, I'd actually seen him, every morning for a few weeks now.

The waitress returned to our table and we all declined refills on our drinks. She eyed the pizza. "Want me to grab a to-go box?"

I shook my head, so she pulled a leather folio with the check from her uniform pocket and left it on the table. I glanced at it briefly to make sure it also included the tab for my crew. We won, so Sinclair Construction paid. If we lost, they could buy their own food and drinks. I tucked my company credit card in the folio and slid it to the edge of the table.

My sister and best friend's stares remained fixed on me.

"Just what I thought," Hope said smugly. "She doesn't know her type at all. She's just being contrary, as usual."

Plum nodded in agreement. "Riley being Riley."

I should have just let it go, but the two of them were such know-it-alls. "My type doesn't wear a hard hat or steel-toe work boots." My words were soft and tentative as my mind conjured up the man I had watched stride in and out of the office building across the street from one of our job sites. I saw him twice a day: once during the morning rush when office workers descended downtown, and again at the end of the workday. "He wears a suit and tie."

Hope's chin hit her chest, while Plum motioned with her hand for me to continue, so I did.

"My type goes to work with a laptop bag slung over his shoulder, not a tool belt slung around his hips, and he looks like he just stepped off the cover of GQ *magazine.*"

I continued to tell them what little I knew about the man who ruled my dreams. "He works with his brain, not his hands."

Plum and Hope continued to gawk at me, but I was unsure whether it was over the type of man I wanted, or the fact that I had a type in the first place.

Plum's eyes narrowed. "Sounds to me like this guy is more than a hypothetical type. Have you met someone?"

I shook my head. Every time he walked past, I fantasized about him finally noticing me, but he was always on his phone. Besides, who would notice a woman in a hard hat and worn jeans, usually covered in grime or concrete dust?

"Well, this is a surprise," Hope said. "I never knew about this type of yours, or that you wanted someone so refined and...don't take this the wrong way, but the total opposite of you."

Neither had I, until I saw him. But it didn't matter. In fact, I felt ridiculous for even mentioning it. Nothing would ever come of my infatuation with a stranger.

"I just wanted to make it clear: Hudson Parker is not, and will never be, the man for me." My gaze drifted to the other side of the room, where he was standing at the bar talking to the guys. Suddenly, he looked over their heads and met my stare head-on. The scrutiny of his dark-eyed gaze sent another shiver through places on my body that shouldn't be responding to anything concerning him. I abruptly turned away and was relieved my dining companions were none the wiser.

Hope pulled out her phone and frowned at the screen. "I'd better get going."

I stifled a yawn with my fist. "Yeah, me too."

"Hold on, before everybody scatters, we're still on for tomorrow night, right?" Plum asked.

"Of course! Do you actually think I'd miss *Hot Mess* after last week's cliff-hanger?" I asked. "I've got to see how Delilah is going to fix this latest mess she's gotten herself into."

Hot Mess was currently the number one show in the country; a true television phenomenon. Every Friday night eyeballs were glued to the screen to see what kind of trouble the series' main protagonist, Delilah Cole, portrayed by Golden Globe–nominee Nova Night, was going to get into. And more importantly, how she was going to get out of it.

Savvy and educated, as well as a style trendsetter, the character of Delilah was the perfect blend of beauty and moxie. Every week, the fictitious business consultant had her choice of the most powerful men in the country, and they all hung on her every word.

Add that scandalous family of hers to the mix, and things got very *messy*, as the show's title inferred.

"It's your turn to play host, Riley. You making pizza?" Plum smacked her lips. "I know we just had one tonight, but it doesn't compare to yours."

I wasn't much on the cooking front, but I made a helluva homemade pizza. Better than the one we'd just eaten, for sure.

"No can do. I won't have time." I made a mental note to stop by Publix's deli on the way home to place an order for a ready-made tray. I could pick it up tomorrow after work. "You're bringing dessert, right?"

"Yep, cake pops. Your favorite," Plum replied.

I smiled. "Bring extra."

"Will do." She turned to my sister. "You have drinks covered, Hope?"

My sister looked up from her phone. "Count me out, guys. I won't be able to make it."

Plum fisted her hands on her hips. "What on earth do you have to do that's more important than watching *Hot Mess*?"

"Dinner with my fiancé's boss," Hope replied. "Rob just texted. It's apparently one of those you-had-better-be-there affairs."

"Oh, I almost forgot. Tammy and Candace aren't coming, either. Tammy's in-laws are in town, and Candace has a Lamaze class," Plum said.

It didn't come as a surprise. Once our single friends became half of a married couple, things changed. Sure, they always vowed our girls' night would go on as before, but despite their good intentions, their newfound marital obligations took priority.

Plum would do the same once she tied the knot on Christmas Eve next year. Hope hadn't even said, "I do" yet, but she'd already started.

Standing, I glanced around the restaurant. Some of the guys had started to filter out, but there were players from both teams still watching the game. I didn't care as long as the ones who worked with me punched the clock on time tomorrow morning. "So do I need to order an entire platter or just a couple of sandwiches?"

"A small platter should do it," Plum said, gathering her things. "Tiffani, Ginger, and Alison are still coming."

Hope shook her head. "Nope, Alison has a big date at some fancy restaurant Saturday night. She took off work tomorrow to have a spa day, because she's expecting Derek to propose."

Girls' night was a big deal to me. I worked mostly with men, and the few women on my crew were mothers who spent their time off the job caring for their kids. They didn't have time for the company softball team or getting together after work.

I sighed as Hope continued to fill us in on Alison and Derek. With everyone coupling up, it wouldn't be long before our girls' night watching *Hot Mess* turned into *girl* night, and I ended up watching it solo. When that happened, I'd have to find a new favorite show, because the thought of sitting home alone watching Delilah Cole juggle her choice of good-looking men was just too damn depressing.

ABOUT THE AUTHOR

A former newspaper crime reporter, Phyllis Bourne
writes to feed a growing lipstick addiction. A nominee for
Romance Writer's of America's 2016 RITA® award and a
two-time Golden Heart finalist, she has also been nomi-
nated for an RT BOOKReviews Reviewer's Choice
Award and won Georgia Romance Writer's prestigious
Maggie Award of Excellence.

When she's not at the computer, Phyllis can be found at a
cosmetics counter spending the grocery money. She lives
in Nashville with an understanding husband, who in one
kiss can discern the difference between a department
store and drug store lip gloss.

 facebook.com/phyllisbournebooks

 twitter.com/phyllisbourne

instagram.com/phyllisbourne

Made in the USA
Coppell, TX
20 September 2020

38332028R00090